Ain't No Mess Like Church Mess

In the Beginning

SHONDRA MITCHELL

ISBN 9781704845104

Disclaimer

This book is a work of fiction, directly from the Author's vivid and multifaceted imagination. All names, characters, events, people, places, things, products, etc. are the products of the author's imagination, or are used fictitiously for entertainment purposes only. Any resemblance to actual persons, living or dead, businesses, companies, events, or locales is entirely coincidental.

Please leave your positive reviews on the website you purchased your book from.

In addition to being an Author, I am also a Certified Life Coach and Motivational Speaker.

Please feel free to contact me if you are interested in any of my services. Also, please like and follow my social media pages listed below.

My email address is authorshondram@gmail.com

Facebook page info

https://m.facebook.com/shondjac

Instagram page info

https://www.instagram.com/authorshondram/

I have 3 other Books (They are all free with Kindle Unlimited)

I Saw the Best in Me (Book)

Paperback ⇓⇓⇓⇓

https://www.amazon.com/gp/aw/d/1515070506/

Electronic formats ⇓⇓⇓⇓

http://www.amazon.com/dp/B0122H02ZQ

Troublesome Times Are Here (Book)

Includes prayers, inspirational narratives, and encouraging words.

Paperback ⇓⇓⇓⇓

https://www.amazon.com/dp/1540447111

Electronic formats ⇓⇓⇓⇓

https://www.amazon.com/dp/B01MY05KAV/

Never Again Will I (Book)

Electronic Formats ⇓⇓⇓⇓

http://www.amazon.com/dp/B079SS4NH5

Paperback ⇓⇓⇓⇓

https://www.amazon.com/gp/aw/d/1984205951/

I create motivational videos on my social media pages everyday called "Lunchtime Lollygag Messages." Please feel free to watch and share them with others.

Thank you so much for your support!!!!

Author Shondra Mitchell

Acknowledgements

I would like to thank God, from whom all blessings flow. I am appreciative of the gifts that He's given me. He does all things good, and He does all things well! I'm especially grateful for my husband Joe. You always believe in me, and remind me I can do all things through Christ that strengthens me. You helped push me out of my comfort zone with this book, so that I can show the world and my readers just how multifaceted I am as a person and Writer.

My J babies, thank you for believing in your Mama! I know you all are watching me, and because of that, I can never give up. Always remember that you have limitless potential, and you can make your dreams come true.

Prologue

WE ALL HAVE sinned, and fallen short of the glory of God. Sin has been prevalent since the beginning of time. It began with Adam and Eve in the Garden of Eden, and continues now in present times. This book is sexually explicit, contains foul language, and speaks of different sins that people commit, such as envy, lust, greed, and more.

I purposely included these things in this book, because before we were Christians, we were humans. And even though we are Christians, a lot of us still struggle with the things that I've mentioned above, and much more. As people, we are flawed individuals. As Christians, we are in constant and continual spiritual battles. These battles can be with lust, our flesh, our past, temptation, and anything else that one may struggle with in their spiritual lives.

This work of fiction was created to remind us that Christians in general, including the most devout and holy Christians, can be overtaken by sin. Those Christians whom you may think have it all together, regardless of their title, may not have it all together. Always be mindful of the fact that no one is exempt from the fiery darts of the enemy.

Your problems and your struggles may not be adultery or fornication, but are you harboring unforgiveness and bitterness towards someone? Are you gossiping and judging others? Are you lying, and using your words to tear people down? Are you doing other things that I haven't mentioned above that is considered sinful?

Sometimes as people, we have the tendency to categorize sin. In God's eyes, sin is sin. As you read this book, I ask that you consider your ways, and check your own heart. It's easy to use a fine-tooth comb to pinpoint the sins of others, but it's not always easy to see and admit to our own flaws and sins when we do self-examinations.

What areas in your life is sin prevalent? What areas in your life do you need more spiritual help and guidance in? Once you realize what the sin/sins are, be humble enough to repent, and get back on the straight and narrow path.

Don't continue to dibble and dabble in sin. Don't continue to slip and slide in sin, and more importantly, don't judge people that sin differently than you. There are times that we judge people for the very things that we've been delivered from, and if we aren't careful, those things can overtake us again. Even the Bible says, "such were some of you," before we made the decision to change our lives.

Please don't change the way that you feel about church, religion, spirituality, church people, church leaders, and life in general. This book is fictitious and for entertainment purposes only. Your spirituality is real and not to be played with.

Be encouraged,

Author Shondra Mitchell

Chapter I

I'VE ALWAYS BEEN an on-point person. I've planned my moves strategically, and every step I make is calculated. Being naked in a car is definitely something that I'm used to, but the blood and the fat lip weren't. I'm freaky, but not that freaky! I don't play that hitting mess when I'm getting it on. I started to feel cold, and when I looked down, I saw that I was naked. I started to try to process the fact that I was naked in the middle of winter in a car, but I just couldn't make any good sense of it.

I started looking for my clothes, and they were nowhere to be found. To wake up in the middle of the night, in the middle of nowhere with my heart racing, left me confused, baffled, and bewildered. I wondered for minutes where I was. It was cold, dark, and I was something that I've never been in the 12 years that me and Leon have been together, I was alone.

How did I get here? I wondered. I looked to the left and right, and all I saw was fogged up windows. I felt something wet coming from my forehead. Before I could look in the mirror to see what it was, blood dropped in my eyes, causing me to become blind for a moment. I rubbed my eyes, which caused blood stripes to get all over my hands.

I looked in the mirror only to see a big gash on my forehead with blood gushing from it. My cheeks had dried up blood stains on them, and my lips were big and swollen, as if I'd been punched in the mouth. I tried to turn the car on so I could turn on the heat and bail. Nothing happened. I turned the key in the ignition again, and all I heard was "click, click, click," when I turned the key.

Seeing that my phone only had a 2% charge remaining, I knew I had to act quickly. I picked up the phone, and voice dialed a number that was familiar to me. This was a number that I called for years, day in and day out. During the good, the bad, and the troublesome times, this was a number that I knew would be sure to answer.

There was a message that came on the phone that said, "Service unavailable." I voice dialed Bae's number again, and this time I got action. "Thank you, Lord," I yelled! The phone rang one time, and then went straight to voicemail. I wanted to leave a message, but I didn't in fear of my phone dying. *What is going on?* I thought to myself. I had to think of a plan B quickly.

My phone is on 2%, I'm alone, I'm cold, and last but not least, my car won't start. I opened the door to see where I was at. The area looked familiar to me, but I just can't understand why I'm here, and more importantly, how I got here.

In the midst of this situation that I find myself in, all I could think to myself was how I've been here countless times, with someone I shouldn't have been here with, doing things that I shouldn't have been doing. I got so scared, because I realized that the place that once bought me so much pleasure and joy, may end up being the place where I take my last breath.

I began to shake, scream, cry, and have a nervous breakdown all at once. In the past, when I'd get myself in a mess, a certain Bible verse came to the forefront of my mind, and it's at the forefront of my mind now. "Be assured, your sins will find you out." I cried out to the Lord. "Lord, where are you?"

All I could think to do was what I do every time my back was against the wall, and that is to PRAY.

"Dear Lord,

I don't know why I'm here, how I got here, or how I'll get out of here, but I know You. I know that You can make a way out of no way. I'm humbly asking You to deliver me from this situation. I know I haven't always done right as a Christian, but I'm asking You not to hold that against me now. Please show mercy towards me, as You've showed mercy towards me countless times before. I don't want to die here Lord, so please send someone to help me out of here. That's all I remember…"

Chapter 2

RING RING RING, buzzed the alarm clock. I turned to my overly loud alarm clock that was flashing 7:00 am, slammed on the snooze button, put a pillow over my face, and rolled back over in disgust. I thought to myself, *that alarm clock is so rude and disrespectful*! I heard rain drops outside, and my cell phone was ringing. I couldn't help but think to myself, *it's too early for this B.S.*

I heard a bunch of thumps coming from the ceiling above me. Those thumps are all too familiar to me, they were the bumps and thuds of my 3 children running around every morning. They couldn't just get up like regular, good, quiet children. They always had to get up like hooligans. I listened closely, and heard them yelling at each other, and then the crying starts.

They all come running down the stairs like a herd of big ol elephants, and one by one, they come in with a different story. "Mommy, Kylie hit me. 'Mommy, she's lyinnnggg," in the whiniest of all whines, said MJ, the youngest of the bunch. JJ, who is the oldest boy, gives his version of the story, and I'm wanting to scream at the top of my lungs," SHUUTTTT UPPPP!!!!"

In the meantime, my husband Leon is curled up sleeping like a damn baby. I am so pissed! I looked over at him, and immediately get an attitude. He wants to be the disciplinarian all the time, but when stuff hits the fan, he acts like he doesn't hear the B.S. that's going down.

I'm bout sick of him. Now don't get me wrong. My bae is a good man, I mean a really good man. He's very nice looking. He has beautiful white teeth that glistens every time he smiles. He smells so good, and keeps a nice krispy cut and shave.

I be seeing all the girls lusting after him, but that right there, that's MINE! We've been together for about 12 years now, and I've never had any problems with other women, cuz he loves me. He loves all this thickness and attitude that comes with me. We do all of the stuff that "relationship goals" couples do, such as holding hands in public, wearing matching outfits with matching Jordan's and Air Max's, and post beautiful family pictures on social media. We have a big house with a lot of land. He has an Escalade and I have a BMW.

Our children are perfect (well at least in my head they are.) I always tell people that they got their good looks from me and my family, and Leon and his family had nothing to do with their DNA at all. They are all brown skinned with smooth caramel complexions like mine. My daughter Kylie who is the middle child, has long curly hair down her back. She has a very exotic look to her. She's so pretty, she doesn't even look like she belongs to us. My boys keep a krispy cut, and have a nice grade of hair as well.

Our children go to the best school, a private school, in which we pay good money for them to get the best education. They have the best of everything, and they don't want for nothing. My husband is an Engineer for a prominent software company here in Memphis, Tennessee, and I am a 5-time New York Times Bestselling Author and National Motivational Speaker.

We get compliments everywhere we go about the beautiful family that we have, and people even call us a power couple. We are the "it" couple amongst all of our friends and family. From the outside looking in, we're the perfect couple. People think we have it all together, but from the inside looking in, that's just not the case. You and I both know that what's shown on the outside isn't always an indication of what goes on in the inside. Truth is, I'm miserable, and I want out!

I want a man that I can go out and have fun with. I can't remember the last time we went out on a date. I got all these beautiful shoes and clothes in my closet collecting dust, because he doesn't want to do anything or go anywhere. I want a man that I can laugh, play, and wrestle with. His idea of fun is reading the Bible.

Now don't get me wrong, I love reading the Bible, but I'd rather go out and spend quality time with my husband. We have the money to do whatever we want, but his focus is on nothing but his job and the church. I want a man that has a sense of humor, and Leon is a hermit that tells corny jokes. We no longer have a companionship or friendship, and the worst part about it all is that no dick is being served. All he does is goes to work and church, and I'm so sick of it.

He and his childhood friend Johnny Reals are the founding Pastors of our church, Mt. Sinai Commissioned Missionary Baptist Church, and they both are super passionate about their calling and their anointing. Johnny has been in our life the majority of time that we've been together, and is literally like family to us. I call him Pretty Boy Johnny (PBJ) cuz he is fine!

He's high yellow with waves and green eyes. He's definitely a good man, and will be a good catch whenever he finally does find a wife. I always tease him about finding a girl, so that he can leave my house. If he's not at the church, then he's up in the office with Leon talking about God and church matters.

I don't mind Johnny coming over, because a lot of times when he comes, he brings food, and the kids love their God Daddy. He plays with the kids more than Leon does, and my daughter Kylie has him wrapped around her little finger. PBJ's and Kylie's bond is even stronger than the bond Kylie has with her own father, and it gets under Leon's skin. I've told him if he took the time to pay attention to his kids, maybe they'd have more respect and love for him.

Sometimes I wish PBJ could be their father instead of their Godfather, because of the way Leon deals with them. To be honest,

Leon is going to find himself single if he doesn't make a change regarding the way he treats me and the kids.

The church has been in existence for a little over a year now, and I'm OVER IT!!! Ever since he and Johnny started the church, he's changed. Our life in general is so boring, and our sex life is nonexistent. I often argue with him because I'm hot, horny, and ready to be screwed!

He makes me feel like he's not attracted to me sexually or physically. I have all these sexy clothes that I've been dying to put on that is no longer appealing to him. Before he started the church, I'd catch him drooling at the sight of my breasts spilling out of my bra and over my shirt. He'd love for me to wear short skirts and high heels so that he can get a "little taste," while we were waiting for our dinner to arrive when we'd go on dates.

Now when I dress provocatively, he tells me to put some clothes on. He says that a woman of God shouldn't be exposing herself. I am a woman of God, but hell, I still like to be sexy for my husband. Since when has it become a sin for a woman to look good and dress up for her man the way he likes to see her, or the way he used to like seeing her?

I always wear lingerie, and literally throw myself on him. When I do that, he turns the other way. When I rub up on him, he tells me to get off him. When I'm prancing around naked making sure everything in the right areas is bouncing, jiggling, and shaking, he tells me to go sit down somewhere. What man wouldn't like that? I'm willing and ready to be at his service sexually at any time, day or night, and he doesn't pay me any attention.

The way he's been treating me has really been hurting my feelings. The last thing that I, or any wife wants to feel at any point of time is that her husband isn't turned on by her any longer. He used to be a big freak. No place nor time was off limits for him. Truth be told, those spontaneous moments of passion was one of the reasons I fell in love with him.

I mean, we've "got it on" any and everywhere. There was something about knowing that at any time, at any moment, we could get caught in our heated love making sessions that just turned me on. The blood rush, anxiousness, and fear that came with those moments were just awesome, and I miss it.

Last week when I told him I wanted to satisfy him on top of the communion table, he looked at me in disgust and asked, "Are you crazy?" I wanted to remind him of the time that he bent me over the toilet seat at a church for a 'quickie' at a friend's wedding. I guess 'Mr. Holier than Thou' got amnesia to the freaky and kinky stuff we used to do on holy grounds.

I want romance, I want foreplay, and I want to be fucked hard! Even though we're both 35, you'd think that he's 55, because he's so damn boring. He lets all his youth and stamina go to waste. I really wish that he'd just go cheat on me with someone else, so I could be rid of his ass once and for all. Just give me my half, and be on your damn way! I've told him that millions of times (in my head of course.) I want a man that's exciting, and stimulates me mentally and sexually. He ain't hittin on nothing, and hasn't been for a while now.

I know you're wondering why I continue to deal with him if he's that bad. I know I can do way better than him, as I got men hitting on me all the time! Truth is, I know my heart is safe with him. He's the man that I've spent the last 12 years with. We've grown together. We've cried together. We've laughed together. We were broke together, and we've built together. I know that he won't cheat on me, as he's a very loyal, faithful, God fearing man, and it seems to be very rare to find younger men nowadays that are faithful to their wives.

I've been praying that things will change between us, but I feel like my prayers are falling on deaf ears. Plus, according to the 'church,' I don't have a valid reason to divorce him, as he's never cheated on me. So, I'm pretty much stuck in this passionless, emotionless marriage with Leon, but scared to divorce him, because I don't want to go to hell.

I can hear people talking about me now. Lord knows I don't need or want that. One thing that I do know for sure is that, "It ain't no mess like church mess." I don't want no mess or no drama in my life at this point, so I grin and bear it. People idolize us and our relationship, and

I don't want to let them down. Even though I don't want to let them down, I feel like I'm settling and lying to myself.

I've been having to rebuke the thoughts of cheating on him, because baby, they're at the forefront of my mind. I feel like if I cheat on him, he'll want to divorce me, and I'll be out of my misery. Sounds like a win/win to me.

Chapter 3

I GO TO CHURCH whenever the doors are open. Not because I necessarily want to be there, but because Leon is so passionate about it. Before he founded the church, I kept telling him that I am NOT preachers' wife material. I have a past that I'd like to keep in the past. Of course, he knows of my past, but if the 'Saints' found out, they wouldn't want me to be their 1st lady either.

See, I love the Lord, but every now and then I likes to get it in! I enjoy my ladies night out sessions with my girls which includes talking about men, reality tv, and all sorts of foolery. I like to get my drink on, and even though I love Jesus, I cuss a little, as you can see.

This church is the 2nd reason why I'm so damn miserable. Me and Leon have really been bumping heads recently because he is talking about quitting his 6-figure job at the engineering company to become a minister full time. Did I mention he gets $5500.00 deposited into our bank account every 2 weeks?

Leon's money comes into my account faithfully every other Friday like clockwork. My income is sporadic and not consistent like his, but when them checks hit the bank, babbbyyy, our account be on swole! I've come to depend on the consistency and amount of pay that he receives, and our whole life is based on it. My income is dependent on who wants to buy books, and who wants to be motivated, and we all know that people can be inconsistent as hell.

Some months I may make between $500.00-$1000.00, and then other months I have made upwards of $10,000.00 if I have events and conferences scheduled. He wants to take over $10,000.00 out of my house every month to work in the 'House of the Lord,' fuck that! We got about 125 members, and they are cheap as hell.

On a good Sunday, the church may bring in a good $500.00 to $600.00, but the average is $125.00-$200.00 a week. He wants me to be happy with the 'measly coins' from the Saints. I ain't never been no bare minimum broad, and I ain't bout to start now cuz Leon wants me to see his vision. Fuck him and his vision. I needs to keep my bag secured.

Speaking of bags, it amazes me how every woman in this church has a designer handbag and red bottoms, but when it's time for them to 'give as they have prospered,' you'd think they're scraping from the bottom of the barrel. They give like the Lord hasn't been good to them. See, I be peeping these lame broads' games. Right before it's time for the offering, they start leaving like the little roaches and rats that they are. One by one, they come give me a kiss followed by lame ass excuses like, "I gotta go to work First Lady, an emergency came up, I gotta leave Sister Bowens, and I'm not feeling well, yadda, yadda, ya."

And I play right into the fakeness, "Bye bitch..... I mean, bye baby, have a great week, be blessed." When deep down inside I be wanting to say, "Fuck you bitch wit yo fake ass." I saw how you were looking at my husband on the low.

Every time I come to this church, I'm disgruntled, and mad as hell. No one would ever be able to tell though, because I put on my fake face. My, "Everything in life is perfect, my God is good, pray about it and voila, everything is fixed face." Leon is good about keeping appearances. He's all for the show. He wants everyone to think we have this happy life at church.

He's always rubbing on me and showing me all the feels at church by massaging my shoulders and rubbing my back, but when we get home, I can't pay him to touch me. He acts like this loving father and plays with the kids at church. At any given time, I see him play boxing and talking to the boys. I'll see him carrying Kylie and showing her love as well.

As a result, the kids love church, because that's the only place and time that they get attention from their father. I on the other hand hate going to church, because that's the place where I'm forced to be what I'm not, and that's fake. I do everything in this church from communion preparation, to cleaning, to printing the programs, to anything else that needs to be done, and I'm tired of doing everything by myself.

I keep asking 'Pastor' if he can get me some help, but he's cheap as fuck, and doesn't want to pay nobody, and don't nobody want to work for free. I've been purposely leaving stuff undone to force his hand to get me some help, but he acts like he doesn't see it. I can't continue to manage a household, try to put out best-selling books, and work in the vineyard of the Lord by myself.

I took it upon myself to ask one of the deacons if he could help me out. Deacon Johnson is one of our most faithful servants, and happily accepted the position to help. As a result, I delegated all the tasks that I do over to him. Deacon Johnson got the 'big head' with his new responsibilities, but I love to see him so passionate about the Lord's work. He takes pride in taking the collection plates to the back to count the tithes and offering with Pastor Johnny.

In addition, he took it upon himself to put security cameras in the church, and to pay for alarm monitoring services out of his pocket, just to ensure our church building is secure at all times. Leon wasn't really feeling it when I told him that I'd delegated my duties to Deacon Johnson. He felt I went over his head, and disrespected him by asking Deacon Johnson for help, versus allowing him to get me help. As a result, we got into a really big argument, and now Leon is mad at me.

The way he's acting is just even more of a reason as to why I want out of this marriage. Relieving myself of these duties will be one less loose end I'll have to tie up when it's time to bail. I'm slowly but surely trying to devise an exit strategy from this church and marriage. Right now, I'm loving Deacon Johnson. I feel as if he's a blessing from God. He's playing right into my hand, and making my life easier, and I'm not mad at him for doing so, even if it does come at the expense of my husband being mad at me. He'll get over it....

Chapter 4

I'M PROBABLY THE weirdest first lady ever. I'm very nice to everyone, but I'm not the first lady type to invite people into my home. I don't cook casseroles and biscuits, and I'm not the type of first lady that will go up to people and introduce myself. I'll speak and be cordial, but I'm not one to start conversations. I have my guard up, especially when it comes to women. I guess I'm that way because I've seen how women are, and watched how they do each other. I know what I've done to other women as well (truth be told.)

I have a few women that I'm cool with, but there is one woman in particular that I just love. Her name is Sister Tricee Johnson. That's my dawg! She's fly, respectable, and just all about her business in general. She's mad dope. Ever since I met her, we cliqued, and it's not too often that I find a woman that I dig, and actually want to be friends with. I love her so much!

I even put her down as an emergency contact to pick up my kids, and I don't trust nobody with my kids other than Johnny. She's a good, single woman, so I'm going to try to hook her up with Johnny, cuz he's a good man who needs a good woman. The 2 of them would definitely make some beautiful babies, and I'm here for it!

From what I hear, my standoffishness is starting to become a problem amongst the ladies in the church. Although people look up to me and respect me, they feel I should be more open and engaging. What they don't know is that I'm in a place where I don't want to be, uncomfortable and angry on the inside.

It's best for everybody when I just stay low key and to myself, cuz my Grandma always told me, "If I don't have nothing nice to say, don't say anything at all." I told Leon, "He betta choose between me being there being myself and not engaging, or me not being there at all," cuz he ain't getting both.

As First Lady, part of my job duties is to counsel. This has to be the only thing that I do like about my position. I like being able to help people with their problems, and I like encouraging and motivating people. Encouraging and motivating others is what I do best, but on the other hand, I have no one to confide in.

When people think your life is perfect, you can't go to them with your issues. I can't tell the very people that look up to me that I'm miserable. I can't let people know that I don't have the perfect relationship that they think I have. As a result, I keep a lot of things to myself, and I suffer in silence.

When I feel like I just can't take it anymore and I'm about to reach my breaking point, I call Johnny. Although I don't like putting people in our business, he's Leon's best friend. They're actually more like brothers, and I confide in him, as he's never told any of our business to anyone else.

My need to vent caused me to pick up my phone and call him. The phone didn't even ring good before he answered. "What up sis?" he asked, after answering the phone. "Oh, you know, same ol same ol," I replied. "So, Leon still ain't doing right huh?" he asked, sounding the least bit interested. "Right, I don't know what else to do bro," I responded.

"I've been telling you for years what to do, but you just too hard headed and won't listen," he said sarcastically. "I'm for real for real," I replied, in an agitated tone. "You're always with the games," I said.

"Come on over to the winning team, I told you that a long time ago," he said laughing.

"Oh, so you with the 'play play' today huh?" I replied. "You know I got to give you a hard time. I don't know sis, you always come to me with this. Have you ever gone and talked to him about how you feel?" he asked. "You do know that the best person to talk to about your relationship problems is the person that you're in a relationship with, right?" he asked, in a serious tone.

"Well, that's where you come into play," I said. "But you aren't in a relationship with me," he said sharply. "I was really hoping that you could talk to him, man to man, and kind of just remind him that he has a good woman that he's about to lose if he doesn't get his stuff together," I said, in a whining tone.

"Girl please. I got into y'all business one time before, and Leon chewed my head off about it. You know I love you to death, but this, I'm going to stay out of. Some battles, you gotta fight on your own, and this is one of them," he said.

"Do you think it's somebody else? I mean, what's wrong with me?" I asked, as I began to cry. "What's wrong with him is a better question Yosh. Any normal man would be happy to have a beautiful, well-endowed woman such as yourself. If it is someone else, it's on the low, cuz he knows not to try me with no foolishness. He knows he can't bring no other women around me, cuz if he does, I'mma hit him with the word of God. I don't condone or play that mess," he said confidently.

"Well, you're my Pastor, and I'm asking you how I should handle this situation?" I asked Johnny inquisitively. "He's not only your husband, but he's your Pastor as well, and you need to go to him with the situation. As always, I'll pray for you. Put ya big girl draws on, and go reignite that fire y'all once had," he said jokingly. "You get on my nerves," I said. "I love you too," he said, before hanging up on me.

Chapter 5

"**B**ROTHER, I CAN'T believe we made it to this position," Leon said to Johnny, as he walked into their office at the church. "Ever since we were little boys, it's been our dream to be Pastors of a church," Leon reminded Johnny. "I definitely do remember man, but this church here ain't bringing us no big money in," Johnny admitted.

"I wanted us to be the founding Pastors of a mega church that would be bringing in millions of dollars a month. This here ain't what I dreamed day in and day out about. I can barely pay my rent. After a while, I'm going to have to move in with you and Yosh," Johnny said, in a frustrated tone.

"Remember, we have to start somewhere. Things aren't gonna just take off overnight, and anything that is big has once started off being small," Leon reminded Johnny. "Yeah whatever, you up in here sounding like Yosh now with all that inspirational and motivational stuff," Johnny said. "It's the truth man," Leon replied.

"Boy, if I can't say anything else about the church, there sho is some finnnnneeee ladies in our church bro," Leon said to Johnny. "Every time Sister Johnson gets up, that booty start shaking like it's nervous. I start getting all types of lustful thoughts. Have you ever had to repent from the pulpit bro?" Leon asked Johnny. "Yep, I sure have," Johnny said laughing.

"Who is Sister Johnson?" Johnny asked. "Tricee, you know, Yosh's girl. The only woman up in there that Yosh probably genuinely likes," Leon told Johnny. "Yosh's homie?" Johnny asked, with a look of confusion on his face. "Man, I'm just gonna be honest with you and let you know that you're dead wrong for that. You got Yosh. She ain't enough for you?" Johnny asked Leon. "She aight, but she's old news. Have you seen Yosh's butt compared to Sister Johnson's butt? I mean Yosh is thick, but Sister Johnson is 'thick is hell,' Leon reminded Johnny.

"She got them big ol juicy titties, flat stomach, and a fat ass. Whenever I look at her, my Johnson goes to acting crazy," Leon admitted. "Man, for her, I'd be willing to throw my whole family away, and that's for real for real," Leon said. "Yo, you dead wrong for that, but she is thick as hell though," Johnny admitted, as they both started laughing.

"Man, if I were you, I would've been sampled off the menu," Leon said to Johnny. "It's a constant struggle for me to keep my eyes off the menu, and an even bigger struggle for me not to sample what's on the menu. When Sister Johnson come hugging me every Sunday wit them big ol jugs, I damn near lose my mind bro," Leon said lustfully.

"I mean, they're so soft, and she be making sure I feel all of them DD's. I know she wants me just as much as I want her. I can just imagine her plump lips wrapped around my dick," Leon said, as he gazed into space. "Wow, you are definitely exaggerating that hug. I ain't never heard somebody getting so much out of a hug," Johnny said, crushing Leon's ego. "Well damn man, can a brother dream?" Leon asked, in a disappointed tone.

"Enough is enough. I'm not gonna sit up here and let you talk about another woman, like you're not married to my sister. Yosh don't deserve that man. You act like Yosh garbage or a bum broad. Yosh fine bro. You need to be focused on her, and her only. Stop living in dreamland, when your reality is right in front of you wondering if you're cheating on her," Johnny said. "Can you imagine how devastated Yosh would be if she knew that you even felt this way about her friend?" Johnny asked Leon in a serious tone.

"You need to get refocused man, and not on Sister Johnson's ass and titties, but on your wife," Johnny said, in an irritated manner. "Man, don't tell me who I need to be focused on bro. You need to be focused on all that fresh meat up in the congregation. You know the church girls be freaks, and I know you're ready to get freaky! Hell, you may even find ya wife up in there," Leon said jokingly to Johnny.

"Don't start with that mess again Leon. You always trying to play matchmaker. You know who I want. You know who I've always wanted, and you know that I know how to get what I want. Yeah, I know, but you gotta stop living in the past my brother. Ever since the breakup, you just haven't been the same. I mean it was over 20 years ago. You have got to move on," Leon told Johnny.

"I know man, it's crazy. I was so in love, and to have it just come to an end so suddenly, straight up broke me. I've never been the same since then, and I was never able to get any closure. I mean, how can a person who loves you just stop dealing with you to go start a family with somebody else?

I get an invitation to the wedding, go to the wedding with a broken heart, and watch the love of my life marry someone else. I hear nothing else after the wedding day for years, and then one day I get a phone call out of the blue talking about how I'm loved, how I'm missed, and how I'm thought of. I just don't get it," Johnny admitted sadly.

"Life ain't right bro, and we all know these women are just as trifling as us men are. I just wanna know when you gon stop living in the past, and start taking advantage of all this new booty that's right in ya face?" Leon asked Johnny, in a serious tone. "I mean, we have a church full of women that are accessible to you, and a lot of them are hot and horny," Leon reminded Johnny.

"You can run through one, and if you don't like her, there's so many more women you can run through. Hell, hit all of em, all of em except Sister Johnson. Sister Johnson is the forbidden fruit. That one right there, I'm saving for myself," Leon said, while licking his lips and rubbing his hands together. "You got all this 'fresh meat' to choose from, but you can't get over ya ex. I just don't get it. I honestly just don't understand you," Leon said, with a puzzled look on his face.

"You wouldn't understand," Johnny told Leon. "You've always been selfish and stuck on yourself. I'm talking to my best friend, telling you how I feel, looking to seek some Godly counsel, and all you can think to say is that I need to bang every woman in the church except for Sister Johnson?" Johnny asked, looking confused. "Bro, you are something else man," Johnny told Leon.

"I just want to live vicariously through you, and you're letting me down," Leon admitted to Johnny. "I don't mean to let you down bro, I'm just trying to make Heaven my home," Johnny told Leon. "Hey man on a serious note, I can't do nothing but respect that," Leon agreed with Johnny.

"Gimme some," Leon said, as he held his hand up in front of Johnny to give him a high five. After the high five, they hugged each other. "I love you bro," Johnny said. "I love you too, but I just want to know which one of dem fine broads is gonna be the first on ya hit list?" Leon asked Johnny while laughing.

"Sister Johnson, the 'forbidden fruit' is going to be the first one on my hit list," Johnny replied jokingly. "Well good, cuz I was just playing about her anyways," Leon said, as if he was uninterested. "Yeah right, if looks could kill, I'd be in Heaven right now," Johnny said, as they both laughed as Johnny walked out of the office to leave the church building.

Chapter 6

After Johnny left, Leon sat at his desk staring at the name tag that reads "Pastor Leon Bowens," and became overwhelmed with emotion. *Today is the day that I step out on faith, give my 2 week notice, and become a full time minister,* he thought to himself. His thoughts were interrupted when his cell phone rang, and he answered the call. "Well hello beautiful," he said. "Hey Bae, we need to talk," I said. "Oh yeah? Talk about what?" he asked. "Just us," I said.

"Leon, what happened to us? We used to be best friends. We used to laugh, joke, play around with each other, and have sex. Do you know how horny I am right now?" I asked him. "Do you even realize that it's been over 7 months since you've touched me? I feel like we are roommates, not husband and wife," I admitted sadly.

"Wow, you trippin Yosh," he said, while laughing. "I'm tripping? All I want is some love and affection from my husband. Is that too much to ask for? Every Sunday you get up in the pulpit and paint this picture like we're the perfect loving couple, and then we get home, and you pay no attention to me or the kids. Quite honestly, I'm sick of it," I yelled at him.

"I got all these sexy clothes that I put on, just so you'll notice me.

I walk around in the lingerie that you bought me, and you don't even pay me no attention. What's wrong with you?" I yelled. The silence in the phone started driving me crazy. "Hellooooo!" I yelled into the phone.

"You done?" he asked sarcastically, while laughing. "Wow! I just poured my heart out to you, and all you can do is be an asshole on the other end of the phone?" I asked. "Call it as you may. There is nothing wrong with me. I just have a strong thirst for God, and that's all I can think about at this point in my life. I want to do His will, and I'm 100% focused on my spiritual walk," he told me.

"I want to serve people, I want to minister full-time, and I ultimately want to make Heaven my home. I know we've had this conversation before, but since the last time we've talked about this, I've decided that I'm going to quit my job, and became a full-time minister," he said. "Oh, so when were you going to tell me?" I asked. "I just did," he responded sarcastically. "You do understand that this financial move will devastate us, don't you?" I asked angrily.

"I'm not worried about it. God will provide, He always does," he said confidently. "Leon, I'm one of the Treasurers of that church. You do understand that even on our good months, we don't bring in enough from the church to pay our mortgage, right?" I asked him sarcastically. "I'm aware of that, but I'm also aware of the fact that I have a wife that's hardworking and a go-getter.

There's been months that you've brought in over $10,000.00 dollars a month. You just have to get your hustle on now more than ever. Hell, if nothing else, this should be motivation for you. You've been bringing in chump change these past few months anyways, and I haven't been complaining, but instead holding us down. It's time for you to return the favor," he reminded me.

"Have you lost your damn mind?" I asked angrily. "Leon, I've told you from day one that this is your vision, and that I will support you. But what I won't do is put in more work to support this 'vision' that you decided to pursue, regardless of how I felt about it. At no point of time did you include me in this decision, but now you want me to bust my ass to help you with something that I had absolutely no voice or say so in?" I yelled.

"You should just continue working, and wait until your circumstances and cash flow are more comfortably in alignment with your vision. Furthermore, I feel like when your vision comes to pass, I'll be left stuck behind like it wasn't me that helped fund your 'vision' in the first place. You're nothing but a dumb ass, and you got me all the way fucked up," I said harshly to Leon.

"You talk like a woman of the world. I knew you wouldn't support me in my efforts, so that's why I made the decision to Pastor full-time without your negativity. This is the Lord's will for my life, and regardless if you're on board or not, it's going to happen," he said sharply.

"Yea, ok whatever," I said. "I don't think that you're making the right decision at this time, and as your wife, I have every right to voice my opinion about this. At the end of the day, this selfish decision that you've made is not going to impact just you, but it's going to impact us, and it's just not fair," I said, with tears rolling down my cheeks.

"This is a 'we' thing, not an 'I' thing," he responded. "I've considered income, you, and our family, and as the head of this family, I've said what I said, and I'm going to do what I'm going to do. Again, whether or not you agree, is something that I can honestly care less about. I'm not asking for your permission or your forgiveness. I have to adhere to God's calling on my life," he said frankly.

"Well, let's just forget about all the dumb stuff for now. Can you make love to me tonight?" I asked boldly. "I'm sorry baby, I'm just not in the mood, but when I am, you'll be the first to know," he said. "Leon you're my husband! Not only have you completely disregarded me and my feelings in this decision that you've made, you're not fulfilling my sexual desires. Even the Bible says that spouses are supposed to give each other their 'due benevolence,' and all I'm getting from you is selfishness, and a smart mouth," I said.

"You are slacking, and I would give you a negative 158 in the husband department right now," I yelled at him. "That's fine, because my conscious is clear, and I'm alright with the Lord. At the end of the day, that's what matters to me," he said, in an arrogant tone. "Honestly, what do you expect me to do to release all this sexual frustration that I have built up?" I asked.

"You said it's been 7 months since I last touched you and had sex with you, is that correct?" he asked me. "Precisely," I said sarcastically. "You've been making due thus far right?" he confirmed. "Unfortunately, I have," I replied. "Well keep doing what you've been doing then," he said nonchalantly. "Will you be able to take me to the airport tomorrow? I'm going to leave my car at my Mom's house after I drop the kids off. They're going to be staying with her, as I have the Essential Conference that I'll be speaking at this week," I reminded him. "Download a rideshare app and get a ride that way, I'll be busy," he said matter of factly.

"Wow," I said, as my heart literally felt like it was breaking. "Do you still love me? Is it another woman, because if it is, we can just end this now," I said sadly. "Yoshi, I really don't have time for this. You interrupted me during my prayer time, and now I'm all upset. You know, the Bible says resist the devil, and he will flee. I knew I should've sent you to voicemail," he said, in an annoyed tone. "Really, I'm the devil now?" I said laughing, just so that I could keep from ugly crying. "You know what, FUCK YOU," I said, while hanging up on him.

Chapter 7

Ya girl is the keynote speaker at the Essential Conference. This is the biggest conference in the brown girl community, and we talk about beauty, men, money, positivity, current events, and motivation. This is something else that I can add to my already popping resume.

Because I love the Lord, anytime I speak at any engagement, I find a church to worship at while I'm traveling. I like to have my mind in a good place, and I'm able generally able to find that peace at other churches that I visit, because Lord knows I sure don't get it from Mount Sinai.

While in the taxi on the way to the airport, I went online and searched for churches in the area I'd be visiting in Texas. I saw many churches, but for some reason Mount Moriah Missionary Church of Hope stood out to me. I'm almost positive that the fine man by the name of William Tucker that graced the front page of the website had absolutely nothing to do with my decision. *Who am I kidding*, I thought, while giggling to myself? He had absolutely everything to do with it!

I bought an outfit with me that I was going to wear on Sunday morning, but after seeing that man, I had to get to the mall to buy a new outfit. Mount Moriah wasn't ready for all of this sexiness that was gonna be hitting the door on Sunday morning. My flight landed safely, and I went to pick up my rental car. As soon as I got to my hotel room, I laid down on the bed and started daydreaming. *Tucker, Yoshi Tucker*, was what I was deep in thought about, before I got startled by the phone ringing. My heart started pounding, and I answered the phone frantically.

"Hellloooo," I yelled into my phone. "Yosh! What's wrong?" Leon asked in a concerned tone. "Ummm nothing," I replied. "Why you sounding like you scared? Everything OK? You got somebody in there with you? Yo, what the hell is going on?" Leon asked frantically. "Umm nothing baby, I just dozed off, and the phone scared me," I replied. "Awww man, you scared the hell outta me sounding all scared and stuff," Leon said.

I thought to myself, *if acting like a damsel in distress is gonna have him acting like he cares, I'm going to be a damsel in distress all the time.* He hasn't shown this much concern for me in God knows when. "Oh, so you do still love me huh?" I asked Leon. "Girl, what are you talking about? You know what it is," he said reassuringly. When he said that to me, tears came to my eyes, because he hasn't expressed any type of love or adoration towards me in a long time.

"Hold on for a minute. I need to wipe my face because you got me up in here crying. I went to the bathroom to wipe my face, and noticed how wet I was down there. "Someone wants to say hi," I told him. "I thought you were by yourself. What types of games are you playing?" he asked annoyingly. I put him on speaker phone and started playing with my pussy. I made it make all these wet swooshy swashy noises. "So, are you going to speak back?" I asked him. "What are you talking about now?" he asked in a frustrated tone.

"Did you hear Kat?" I asked excitedly. "Who, what are you talking about?" he asked, sounding mad irritated. At this point, I was so disappointed. He took something that was so special to me, so special to us, and ruined it. You see, whenever we were away from each other, we'd have phone sex. A part of our phone sex would be hearing from 'Kat,' his nickname for my goodies.

Now at this point, I'm just down right offended. He named her, but when I tell him to say hi to her, he's going to act like he doesn't know who she is. "Ohhhh," he said, after a long period of silence. "Nah girl, I ain't even on that, he replied, sounding uninterested.

"I was really just calling to see if you made it there safely, you know, since you didn't call me to let me know when you got there," he said quickly, as if he needed to get off the phone. "Wait, I gotta ask you a question," I said. "I gotta work on Sunday's lesson, so I'll holla at you later," he said. "Goodnight," I said sadly. "Yeah," he responded, before he hung up. I started crying uncontrollably, until I cried myself to sleep.

Chapter 8

"I GOT HER TAKEN care of, so we won't have to worry about her interrupting us," Leon told the strikingly beautiful lady that was laying naked next to him in his hotel bed. "Good, cuz I don't need nobody stopping me from doing what I'm about to do to you Pastor," she said seductively.

"How much you charging these days?" Leon asked her. "Generally, I charge $400-$500.00 an hour, depending on what you want. But for you, I have to charge $1000.00 per hour, and from what I did to you the first time I met you for free, you know it's worth every penny," she said arrogantly. "Why are you over charging me?" he asked, in an offensive manner.

"You're jive kind of a low-key high-profile man. Being with you is very risky, and if we get caught, it's going to be a big deal. People are going to be talking about it, so I just need to make sure that it makes sense financially," she replied.

"Do you have cash app?" he asked her. "I sure do," she replied quickly. "What's your cash app name?" he asked her. "Mzwetpussy," she replied. "Naw, forreal girl, what's the name?" he asked her again. "That is the name," she said, while laughing. "Girl you something else," he said, while logging into his online bank account to check his available funds. "Hmmm," he said, while looking at the balance of $212.36 in his personal account, and $5612.72 in the Mt.Sinai account.

"What's wrong? You can't afford me?" she asked him sarcastically. "Hell yeah I can afford you," he said, while transferring $1000.00 from out of the Mt. Sinai account to his personal account. "I got my cash app up right here, and it's done," he said confidently. "Great, now let's get started," she said, after receiving the deposit notification on her phone.

"You have no idea how I've been feenin for you girl. Ever since the 1ˢᵗ time I laid eyes on you when I was driving down Martin Luther King, I had to turn around and come back to get you. You just turned me on. When I invited you in my car, you smelled so good. And then you pulled my dick out and started sucking it while we were driving down the street in broad daylight. I couldn't believe it. You're just so spontaneous and fun, and I dig that about you," he said excitedly.

"Ever since that time, I'm no longer attracted to my wife. I haven't touched her in over a year, all because of you. You pulled a disappearing act on me, and changed your number. I rode up and down MLK several times daily, for almost a year looking for you. To be honest with you, you broke my heart. I haven't been the same since," he sadly admitted.

"I'm so sorry," she said. "This life as a street walker isn't easy, and I don't stay in the same locations every day. Regrettably, I was still out there though," she said, with her head hung low. "I hated what my life had become. I get sick of having sex with men and women for money.

I was feeling so down, that I considered suicide. I started praying and asking God for direction, and something in me led me to your church," she admitted. "I came in there trying to find God, and I found you again," she said, as she started rubbing on his chest.

"You never told me you were a Pastor, so you can imagine the embarrassment that I felt within my soul when I walked in and saw you in the pulpit preaching. I thought to myself, this is a God thing, because it was too much of a coincidence. This must be God's will for our lives," she said skeptically. "Well, I'm glad we're back together again. I've been saving myself for you baby. I've been celibate for you," he told her.

"Ever since my encounter with you, my conscious won't let me touch my wife," he explained. The first time I did touch her after meeting you, I was just imagining she was you. I can't even get hard from her anymore. As bad as it sounds, I'm just not into her any longer. Can't you tell by the way that I was talking to her on the phone that I'm not into her any longer? Our relationship is dead, it's over. I just want to be with you," Leon told her.

"Have you told her all of this? Does your wife know how you feel?" she asked. "Yesssss!" Leon yelled. "I don't mean to yell, but I'm just so sick of her. All she does is yell, nag, and complain. I've asked her time and time again for a divorce. She is refusing to sign the papers. I wanted to be out of this relationship like yesterday. She keeps crying and begging me to stay with her. She's trying to convince me to stay with her for the kids. I don't really care about her or those kids. Truth be told, I don't even think they're my kids," Leon admitted.

"Are you forreal?" she asked. "Yeah Kat, I'm dead serious," he answered. "Kat?" she repeated after him. "Who the hell is Kat?" she asked, with mad attitude, as she got up and started to put her clothes back on. "Kat is you baby," Leon said. "Kat is the nickname that I just gave you, he said, while trying to calm her down. "Where did that name come from though? It's mad random," she said. "You got that fat wet pussy. She's Kat," he said, as he went down and started sucking on 'Kat.'

"I'm so scared to be here with you Pastor. I don't want to go to hell, but I want you just as much as you want me," she said, as she was pushing his head away from her private area. I guess we can always repent, right Pastor? I mean, what if someone from the church sees us together? What if your wife finds out about us? What will we do?" she asked.

"We will worry about that if and when we need to worry about that," he replied sarcastically. "But for right now, we are just going to enjoy the moment," he said, as he placed his big body on top of hers, and slowly inserted his raw 'manly' part into her raw 'womanly' part.

He gently kissed her on her neck, and all over her body. She moaned in pleasure, as he stroked in and out. With slow continuous strokes, she whispered in his ear, 'I'm the devil.' That turned him on even more, because he started stroking and going in and out harder until he just couldn't take it anymore, finally releasing himself into her. As soon as he got off her, she rolled over towards him and started sucking on his soft penis.

"It's a wrap! Gimme a few hours," he muttered, while trying to get his penis out of her mouth. "The devil is good at what she does," she replied seductively. "Now shut up, and let me suck ya dick," she demanded. "Yes ma'am," he replied. As she started sucking again, he got harder and harder. She got off the dick and started praying.

"Dear Lord,

Please forgive me as I have sinned. I have engaged in sexual activities with my Pastor, and I have enjoyed each and every minute of it.

In the name of Jesus,

I pray,

Amen."

"Amen," he replied.

She then put his dick back in her mouth. He couldn't take it anymore, and blasted off in her mouth. She took it out of her mouth, and started jacking his manhood all over her face and breasts.

When she got it all, she then rubbed the nut on her nipples and licked them. Pastor laid back in amazement, and thanked her for a job well done. "You know we both going to hell for what just happened, the prayer, and the fact that we both enjoyed it so much," he said while laughing. "As long as we're together, I'm good with hell," she replied.

Chapter 9

ONCE AGAIN, I was rudely awakened after the phone startled me. "Hellooo!" I answered in an irritated tone. "Who I need to go cut?" the voice on the other end said. "Tricee girl, you crazy!" I said while laughing. "Cuz you know I'm going to war over you," Tricee said. "First of all, I was sleeping good until you rudely interrupted me. Second of all, heyyyy boo!" I said, as we both busted out laughing.

"Naw but for real, who I need to go cut?" Tricee asked, in a serious tone. "Nobody," I said. "Well good," she responded, cuz you know I'll be on the first thing smokin about mines. "I know you love me, and I thank you for always having my back," I told her. "Knew dat," I wouldn't have it any other way, she said.

"Soooo, why you gotta attitude friend?" she asked. "Leon is getting on my nerves," I told her reluctantly. "I really don't think he's into me anymore, friend. I also don't think it's another woman though," I said. "What?" Tricee said. "Yeah right. He literally worships the ground you walk on. Every time he looks at you, you can just see the love in his eyes," she said, in a reassuring tone. "Well I'm glad you can see it, cuz I damn sure can't," I replied.

"I'm pretty sure it's just some type of misunderstanding," Tricee said. "Have you talked to him about how you feel? I mean, where's all this coming from? Y'all are literally relationship goals, and I'm mad confused that you feel this way. Is there something that you haven't been telling me? I feel like I've been left in the dark about some things," Tricee said.

"I mean, since I've known you, I've never heard you complain or say anything bad about him," Tricee said to me. "I mean, we're good, he just acts like he doesn't like me anymore, and I'm not feeling that," I said sadly. "I got all this 'thick thick,' and he doesn't even want it. He never shows admiration for me, other than when we are at church. When we go home, he acts like I don't even exist," I whined.

"Between me and you Tricee, I'm miserable as hell, and I want out. I can't get a divorce because he hasn't cheated on me. All he does is talk about that church and the Lord. I'm bored as can be. Our relationship is passionless. We don't go anywhere anymore. We don't have fun. The only thing that is good about him is that he has that hefty deposit coming into my bank account every two weeks. Ching Ching!" I said, as we both laughed hysterically.

"But for real for real, I'm miserable. I just wish he'd go cheat on me already, so I can get out of this lifeless marriage, get me some spousal support, and not have a guilty conscious while doing so," I said sadly. "Oh now you tripping for real Yosh," Tricee said. "Is he really that bad? You got you a good man. One of the best men that I know.

If you let him go, one of them ladies at the church gonna scoop him up real quick Yosh, and you know you don't want nobody else to have him," Tricee said. "You don't know a good man is in demand nowadays?" Tricee asked me.

"Yes I do know," I responded to Tricee. "Is that supposed to make me feel better about the situation though?" I asked sarcastically. "No, but let's get real here. Everything that you told me sounds like it can be fixed by just talking to him. Other than what you've told me, has anything else happened?" she asked inquisitively.

"Ok, tell me what you think about this," I said to Tricee. "He calls me earlier to make sure I got in ok. I tell him I did. Now anytime I travel, I'll start playing with my pussy, cuz you know I got that wet wet," I said to Tricee. "Right," Tricee responded, as we both burst into laughter. "I can't stand you," Tricee jokingly yelled to me.

"Well any who, I started playing with myself while on the phone with him, and told him Kat wanted to speak with him. "Kat?" Tricee asked, sounding confused. "Y'all be having threesomes First Lady?" she whispered in the phone. "Noooo silly," I replied. "Kat is the name of my stuff," I said.

"Cuz I was about to say, "What types of freaks do I have as my spiritual leaders?" Tricee jokingly said, as we both laughed. "I let him talk to Kat, and he gon ask who Kat is, like he didn't give her the name in the first place. I was so upset and sad," I admitted to Tricee. "Are you serious, best friend? Now that's bad," she said. "Right, now you understand and see why I say there's a problem?" I asked defensively.

"I do, but at the end of the day, I really think you should just talk to him about it. I mean, I don't think that the things you said are divorceable reasons, ya know," Tricee said. "I mean, I guess," I replied. "Well, you know ya girl is here for you, and I feel so blessed that you opened up to me in this manner. I know you are a very private person. The fact that you've opened up to me makes me feel even more closer to you sis," Tricee said.

"Anytime you want to vent, laugh, cry, or just talk, know that I'm here. Hell, I ain't got no man over here in my little ol miserable world, so I'm always here for you. Don't be keeping stuff like this to yourself, when you got a bestie like me to talk with you through these things," Tricee reassured me. "Yea, you are right," I admitted to her.

"I'm sorry for keeping this from you, but me and him have a united front like we're 'relationship goals,' when actually, we're 'divorce reality.' It's hard to admit that reality to others, but I love and trust you, so I won't leave you in the dark any longer. I know I don't have to tell you not to say nothing, but don't say nothing," I said to Tricee.

"Girrrlll, you done tried my whole life. You have literally just offended me," Tricee told me, as her voice started cracking. "Nooo, I didn't say that to offend you by any means, but you know how I feel about my personal business, and I don't want anyone to know about this," I told Tricee.

"Whatever, the damage is still done, but I guess I forgive you," Tricee said. "Thank you so much. I would never hurt you, and you know that," I told Tricee. "Likewise. You're my bestie and my sister, and I'll never hurt you either, Tricee said to me. "I gotta run, but I want to pray with you before we hang up," Tricee told me.

"Dear Heavenly Father,

I come to You on my bestie's behalf. She and her husband are experiencing some difficulties in their marriage now. Please strengthen them both at this point of time. Please help them to communicate and work out their issues, so they can be a happy family again. Please help me to be a source of strength and comfort for my bestie during this time, and please restore their marriage back to a state in which it will be better than it has ever been.

In the name of Jesus,

I pray,

Amen"

"Amen! That's why I love you so much. I've never had any friends that stopped our phone conversation just to pray for me," I admitted. "That's cuz you were used to messing with them frauds," Tricee said. "You got you an official chick on ya team now," Tricee bragged. "Well, I'm blessed to have you sis," I told Tricee. "Well, I know your time is valuable Mrs. Life Coach and National Bestselling Author, so I'm gonna let you go, so I can get back to my single, boring life," Tricee said.

"Thank you so much! Over the phone hugs," I said to Tricee. "Ummm hmmm," hugs chick, Tricee responded, before she hung up.

Chapter 10

"HUSBANDS, LOVE YOUR wife as Christ loves the church. Husbands, when we learn to love and appreciate our wives, we'll see that our lives will become better. A man is not a man, unless his wife can say that he has been a good husband and father. Your wife is your help mate," Pastor Tucker said. "She wants to feel loved, valued, and appreciated," he yelled to the crowd from the pulpit. *I didn't come here to hear this mushy stuff,* I thought to myself, while walking past the people that were on time for the lesson.

I sat at the end of the row next to a very homely looking woman. I glanced down at her shoes, and they looked like they had seen better days. She looked at me as I was sitting down, and smiled at me. I smiled back, and focused back on the fine man in the pulpit. I had no clue as to what he was saying, because my lustful thoughts took me to his bedroom, and I zoned out to a place full of hot, steamy, passionate sex.

"You see, I love and adore my wife," he screamed. When I heard that, I snapped back into reality. "She means the world to me. I don't know how I would have made it this far without her," Pastor Tucker said about his wife. I wondered to myself who the lucky lady was. A lot of women were smiling, as if they would love to be his wife, so it was hard to tell.

"I like to show my baby off from the pulpit," he said proudly, as the crowd started clapping and cheering. "Baby, stand up," and show them who you are, he commanded. I turned around looking, because I had to see who this chick is that stole my man from me. After a moment, the bum sitting next to me stood up. She had a big smile full of pride and joy on her face, and the audience clapped and cheered even harder as she stood up. I immediately started getting sick to my stomach, because I couldn't believe that a fine man like him would speak so highly of this homely looking bum sitting next to me.

I looked back up at her again, and I started to feel jealous of her. I actually hated her in that moment. I couldn't understand how she could be so ugly and bummy, but have her man shower her with praises. I mean, I feel like I deserve to get that same type of public praise from my husband that she was getting from her husband, if for no other reason, because I'm cute and dress nice.

"You can sit down now baby," he told her. As she went to sit back down, she tripped on my foot, and started to fall backwards. I broke her fall, and helped her sit down. "Wow, thank you so much my Sister," she said to me. "I would've been so embarrassed if I would've fallen," she admitted, as we both chuckled about it. "No problem at all," I said to her. I happened to look at her after she got settled into her seat, and she was crying. I saw sadness in her eyes.

At that moment in time, I started to feel horrible. I mean just 10 minutes ago, I hated everything about her because of the way her husband loved her. I then realized that no matter how she looked, she is still a person with feelings. Maybe the tears that she was crying were happy tears, but with a man that fine, I believe that the tears that she cried weren't happy tears.

I can't believe that I am guilty of doing exactly what I preach to other women about not doing, and that is hating on each other. At any one of my speaking engagements, I'm telling a room full of women that they need to be happy for other women. I'm encouraging them to celebrate and congratulate their sisters, versus hating and being jealous of them.

I just realized I'm a big hypocrite, which made me feel even worse. *How can I encourage others to do what I don't do?* I started wondering to myself. At this point of time, tears started running down my face, and I knew that I needed to get this negative spirit up off of me quickly. I did what I always do in times of trouble, I prayed.

"Dear Lord,

Please forgive me as I have sinned. I have unjustly judged this woman sitting next to me, all because she has what I don't have at this point, and that's a loving husband. Please help me to remove these feelings of envy and jealousy from my heart, and allow me to humble myself so that I can learn from her. Please help me to extend love and kindness towards her, and not ill will or bitterness.

It's not her fault that my husband doesn't want me any longer, and I shouldn't treat her as if she's to blame for the breakdown in my marriage, as she has absolutely nothing to do with it.

In the name of Jesus,

I pray,

Amen."

After I prayed, I felt a lot better. My mind was clear, and I was able to concentrate on the last portion of the sermon.

"I do realize that there are couples in the sanctuary that are experiencing marital difficulties. If I'm speaking to you, I just want to remind you to be encouraged. God has not bought you and your spouse this far to leave y'all. He can fix the unfixable. Don't let Satan destroy what was meant for your good! Use today to restore your relationship with the person you love," Pastor Tucker said, with so much feeling and passion.

At that point, I started crying again. I started to think about Leon, and where our relationship stood. I love this man with my whole being, and deep down inside, I just want us to go back to loving, sexing, and having fun with each other again.

Even though I'm still mad with him about how he left the conversation last night, I made a commitment to call him as soon as church let out. I want to express how I feel, and give him the opportunity to do the same. After Pastor Tucker finished his sermon, the choir sang a few encouraging songs, and my spirit was at an all-time high. I can't remember the last time that I felt this spiritually motivated after attending a church service.

After the service was over, I turned to First Lady Tucker and gave her a great big hug. I introduced myself to her, and gave her a VIP ticket to the conference that I will be speaking at this week. I let her know I wanted her to be my special guest. She put her head down and looked as if she was going to cry. "Are you ok Sister Tucker?" I asked her.

"I am, God is just so good. I was praying about going to the conference. When I went to buy the tickets, they were all sold out. Next thing I know, an angel comes and sits next to me this Sunday morning, and blessed me with a VIP ticket to the event," she said, looking surprised. "Girl, that ain't nothing but a God thang," she said, as we both chuckled. "Won't He do it?" I asked, as we both gave each other a high five.

"Well, I'm going to get going now my sister. Will I see you at the conference?" I asked her. "You sure will," she responded. "God's got a blessing with my name on it, and I'm gonna be there to receive it," she said.

"Thank you so much for visiting this morning. You are such a breath of fresh air, and I don't know why, but I feel like we are going to become really good friends," Sister Tucker said. "I have that same feeling too," I said, lying convincingly to her. *She's somebody I definitely wouldn't want to be friends with. She seems to be weak, and I don't like her style of dress*, I thought to myself.

I started walking towards the door, and she started to follow me. "I want to introduce you to my husband," she said. When she said that, my heart started pounding, and I became very nervous. I didn't want what I was thinking about him to show up on my face, especially in front of his wife.

"Oh ok. I would love to salute any man who publicly shows his wife adoration, love, and appreciation. I've visited a lot of different congregations in my life, and I haven't seen that very often. You're such a lucky lady," I told her. As we were walking towards the door, someone called Sister Tucker's name. "Hold on a minute," she shouted to the person who called her. "Honey, I want you to meet this nice lady," she said, as we met him at the door. "She gave me a VIP ticket to the conference this week. She's the keynote speaker," she proudly told him.

"I'll be right back," she told her husband and I, as she walked in the opposite direction to see what the person wanted that called her. "Nice lady huh? Does nice lady have a name?" Pastor Tucker asked inquisitively. While standing there waiting for me to say my name, he extended his hand to shake my hand. "Yoshi Bowens is my name," I replied.

"So, why are you looking at me like you want to fuck me?" he asked, like he could read my mind. "Excuse me?" I asked, as I rolled my eyes with mad attitude. "Is that how you greet a sister in Christ?" I asked sarcastically. "I mean, good morning sister," he said, while correcting himself. "Keynote speaker?" he said, changing the subject. "That means you're beautiful, educated, and you're confident. Sounds like you'll be the perfect wife," he said, as if he wasn't already a married man.

"I'm flattered, and I thank you for the compliment Pastor," I replied. I removed my hand from his, which he was holding the whole time. I couldn't do anything but stare at him. He was tall with big muscles, bald headed, and he had a deep, sexy voice. The sound of his voice alone aroused me. This man turned me on in 2.2 seconds.

I wondered if he could smell how wet I was, because my underwear was soaked. I wondered if the passionate love making scene I had going on in my head was communicated to him some type of way. *Could others see the lust that I have in my eyes for this man?* I wondered to myself.

"And what did you say your husband's name was again?" Pastor asked me. I raised my eyebrows in confusion, because I wondered why he quickly changed the subject. I then saw his wife coming up on the side of us, causing me to understand why he changed the subject.

"Leon," I replied quickly. "Pastor Leon Bowens." I said nervously. I wondered to myself how much of our conversation his wife heard.

Judging from the big grin on her face, I began to calm down, because it was obvious she didn't hear any of it. "I'm so glad that you two are getting acquainted. I don't know why, but I feel like you're going to be an intricate part of our life. I'm just getting this vibe from you that I like. I feel like you are someone that will be my lifelong friend, someone that I can trust, and someone that I can depend on," she said confidently.

"I'm glad that you feel that way, because that's just the type of woman that I am. I love women, and I especially love my sisters in Christ," I responded. "Sister Bowens, in all honesty, my wife has been having a hard time trying to find someone that she can connect with. We are new in our ministry, and the other preachers' wives are all cliqued up, so she's kind of feeling like she doesn't belong," Pastor Tucker admitted.

"Honey, did Sister Bowens tell you that she's a preacher's wife as well?" Pastor Tucker asked his wife. "Get out of here," she yelled in excitement. "I actually am, so I completely understand how you feel about fitting in," I told her. "I knew it was a reason why I love you so much," Sister Tucker said to me. "I mean, I don't even know you, but I love you," she said joyously.

"I think she's what we've been praying for," Pastor Tucker told his wife, as he was standing there looking at me lustfully. As he was speaking, I felt this tingling sensation go through my body, and I wanted to get going before his wife picked up on my attraction towards her husband.

"Well, I have been known to be the answer to a lot of people's prayers, so that may just be the case," I responded, in a playful manner. I started feeling my heart pounding rapidly again, and I got really nervous. There was an awkward silence amongst the 3 of us, and I started to feel uncomfortable. "Well, it has been so nice talking to you guys, but I gotta get going to prepare for this week's conference," I said, as I started walking away.

"Let me go get my keys and my purse, and I'll walk you to the door," Sister Tucker said, as she walked away. I went to extend my hand to Brother Tucker, and he pulled me close to him. He started stroking my hand and kissing my neck. I could have just passed out on the floor right then and there, as my knees got weak. I let his hand go, and pulled away from him.

I started to walk away from him slowly, but because he's so fine, I had to turn around to get one last glance. It's almost like he was waiting for me to turn around and admire his "fineness" again, because when I turned around, he grabbed a handful of his meat, bit his bottom lip, and started pumping back and forth.

I tripped over something on the floor, but immediately caught my fall when his wife yelled out to wait for her. "It was a pleasure meeting you my sister. Feel free to come back and visit us whenever you want to. We want you to know that you aren't a stranger, but you're amongst family.

We love you girl," Pastor Tucker said, in a genuine manner. "We sho do. You have been such a breath of fresh air, and I can't wait to get all this motivation and encouragement that you gonna be serving at the conference," she said, as we were walking out of the building.

"I can't wait to have you as my VIP guest either. Here's my card with my contact information on it. Please text me when you are on the way, so I can be on the lookout for you," I told her. "I will," she responded excitedly, as we hugged each other and said our goodbyes.

On the way back to my hotel room, there were so many thoughts going through my mind. I couldn't stop thinking about how good it felt when Pastor Tucker was kissing me on my neck, and I couldn't help but wonder how his lips would feel all over my body.

I wondered if they were swingers, cuz they both acted like they wanted me. Hell, if they are, I gotta let her know I don't share my man. I want her husband all to myself! I went back to my hotel room, and passed out with a smile on my face, which is something that I haven't done in a long time.

Chapter 11

"Good morning beautiful," a familiar yet unfamiliar voice said on the other line waking me up. "Morning," I replied, with mad sarcasm and skepticism. "Why are you trying to act like my voice isn't implanted in your head? Ever since you left me, my voice and that kiss has been replaying over and over again in your mind," he said confidently.

I chuckled to myself because he wasn't lying. I knew damn well who it was. Ever since I left him, he's been the only thing I've been able to think about. Since meeting him, Leon and I have gotten divorced, and me and the kids are living happily ever after in Pastor Tucker's house, well that's how the story is playing in my head anyways.

"Hmmm?" I replied. "Well since you're going to play dumb dumb, it's Pastor Tucker. I'm going to let you have this round of dumbness, but there will not be another. The next time I call you, I need to hear more excitement in your voice," he said sternly. "Umm, yes sir," I replied.

His sternness hurt my feelings, but it also turned me on, all at the same time. I decided to play into his hand, and let him feel like he has a little control. "Oh, I'm so sorry Pastor, I didn't mean to offend you. It's just early, and I never gave you my phone number, so you're the last person that I would've expected to be calling me," I responded innocently.

"I know this is awkward, but I must be honest with you. I saw your business card in my wife's purse, so I wrote down your number to call you. Please forgive me if I've overstepped my boundaries, but I really could use some of your help and expertise to help some of the ladies in the church," he said.

"I know that you're busy getting prepared for the conference, but do you think that you could make some time to sit down with me and my wife over a lovely dinner? I want to brainstorm over some ideas with you as to how we can help the women to realize that they should be walking in their God given purpose," he said.

"I'd love to set up a workshop for them maybe on a monthly basis, in which you can come and speak with them. I've checked your credentials and quite honestly, I'm impressed. I think you're just what we need to help our women see the best in themselves, so they can be their best for God," he explained.

"Well I'm quite flattered Pastor, but I have to be honest with you regarding this. I've worked very hard to build my platform and business, and my time is very valuable. Even though we are sisters and brothers in Christ, I want to be transparent and let you know that I don't work for free, even if it is in the name of Jesus," I chuckled.

"Who asked you to work for free?" he asked sharply. "Let me tell you something about life and business in general. When someone wants you, they'll pay what they need to pay to get you. You're so busy telling me about what you won't do, that you're not allowing me to tell you about what I'm willing to do," he said sternly.

"You're about to let that cute mouth you got talk you right up out of your blessings," he said sarcastically. "You definitely were going to underbid yourself, I can promise you that. You don't know what I got in store for you," he said sternly.

"I'm sorry Pastor, no ill will intended," I responded. "I see you're going to be a piece of work," he said, while laughing. "There's a really nice steakhouse in the area called Laudy's. Hold on for a minute," he said very softly. I heard a little click, and then he started talking to someone else.

"Hold on dear, I'm talking to my friend Stephen from college. He says hello, and he can't wait to see you again," he said to the person in the background. I heard a woman's voice in the background, but I couldn't make out what she was saying.

She must've come closer to him, because it started to sound like she was on the phone as well. "Go put on something sexy that you know I'd like to see you in," he told her. "Yes Big Daddy," I heard her reply. "Big Daddy's coming," he said excitedly. I heard the click noise again, and then he came back on the line. "I'm so sorry about that my sister," he said, in an apologetic tone. "No worries, I know that you're a busy man," I replied.

"One of the members called because her son went to jail. She wants me to come to the jail to pray with her. I can send you the directions to the restaurant if you need me to. Let's meet there tonight at 7, and we'll finish the conversation then," he said, as he rushed me off the phone. "Sounds good, and I'll see you all then," I replied. "Yep, we'll be there, Lord willing," he said.

Chapter 12

I WENT BACK TO the mall to find an outfit fitting for the occasion. While looking at a cute maxi dress, I started thinking about Sister Tucker, and how I should dress modestly for her. I picked the perfect dress that had just enough cleavage to show Brother Tucker what I'm working with, yet enough dress to be respectful towards Sister Tucker.

I left the mall, and went back to the room to take a nice hot shower. All I could imagine was Pastor Tucker being in the shower with me, rubbing and kissing on me succulently. I took the shower head off the hook, and put it on maximum pressure. I let the water hit my clit, and imagined making love to Pastor Tucker until I nutted on myself, right there in the shower. *Ewww, you nasty*, I thought to myself, while laughing. I rushed out the shower, dried myself off, put on some smell goods, and got dressed to meet with my man.

I pulled up to the restaurant, and valet parked the rental car. I walked up to the restaurant door switching and swaying like I owned the place. *I'm bout to see my man,* is all I could think to myself, while walking up to the hostess stand. "A table for 3 please," I politely said. I looked around the restaurant to see if I could find Pastor and his wife, and they weren't there. I took my seat and pulled my phone out. I couldn't dare let Pastor see me sitting here looking so eager and desperate, waiting to see him.

Generally, at a meeting like this, I'd order a cocktail, but today I just settled for water. I wanted to make sure I made a good impression on Pastor and First Lady. While waiting, I went to search the church's name on the internet. I located a social media page which had 5 stars and raving reviews.

One review said, "Pastor and 1st Lady Tucker have helped me so much throughout my spiritual journey. I don't know where I would be without them." Another review said, "That Pastor Tucker is something special. He knows how to make you feel good, and encourages you to use your God given talents. When I saw God given talents, I couldn't help but wonder if he's got a big dick.

I bet he does, and with those lips of his, I know he'll know how to use his mouth to satisfy me, I thought to myself while laughing. At that moment, my mind just went somewhere that it shouldn't have, and once again, I found myself lusting over this man, who just happens to be somebody else's husband, and a man of the cloth.

Can he just hurry up and come already, so we can get this over with? I thought to myself. At this point, my pussy is wet again, I'm starting to get nervous, and I just want to get out of here. I stood up to go to the bathroom to freshen up, and a god comes walking in. "Leaving so soon?" he asked, as I was walking towards the bathroom pretending like I didn't see him. "Oh no, I'm just going to the ladies' room," I responded politely.

"Well hurry back, I don't like waiting," he said. "And this is coming from the person that just had me waiting for 45 minutes," I said to him playfully. I went in the bathroom stall, hung my purse on the hook, put my face into my hands, and let out a quiet scream. My heart was racing, and I started shaking. *Where the heck is his wife? Am I going to be able to control myself*, I wondered. I came here to eat dinner, but I wanted him to be my dinner. My palms were sweating, and I became so nervous. I did the only thing that I could think to do in that moment, and that is to pray.

"Dear Lord,

I come to You for strength right now. I am in the midst of a fine man, your son, so You know he's fine. I'm weak, and feeling overtaken by temptation. I want him so bad, but I'm a married woman and he's a married man. Please help us to remain focused on your good work, and not on the work of our flesh. Please help us to resist temptation, and help us to remember that we are here for You and your work, and not for each other.

In the name of Jesus,

I pray,

Amen."

After I prayed, I left out of the bathroom stall. I went to the mirror to put on some fresh lipstick, popped some gum in my mouth, and sprayed on some perfume. I left the bathroom, and watched him watching me as I walked across the room. I don't like the fact that he makes me so nervous, as I'm always a bold and confident person.

"Where is First Lady? I was looking forward to seeing the both of you tonight," I said, as if I wasn't happy that she wasn't there. "Well, she had some business that she had to tend to, and wasn't able to make it. Is that okay?" he asked.

"Oh absolutely," I replied. "Thank you for inviting me out to dinner Pastor, this was really nice and unexpected. So what is your specific vision for working with the ladies in your congregation?" I asked. "To be honest with you, the only vision that I have right now is my dick in between your legs, passionately making love to you," he said charmingly. "Excuse me?" I said, acting as if I was offended, when in all actuality, it didn't sound like a bad idea.

"Oh, I'm sorry sister, did I offend you?" he asked, as if he were innocent. "Actually, you did offend me," I said, trying to act like I had integrity and standards. "My sincerest apology. It's just that you're so beautiful, and the way that you're dressed with your breasts out, caused my mind to go elsewhere," he said seductively.

"If you were me, could you blame me? You're a preacher's wife, and generally preachers' wives are covered up and more modest then how you're dressed, so I just kind of took it the wrong way," he said, trying to talk his way out of offending me. "Again, I apologize," he said, looking sad.

"No worries, but I'm here on business, and to be honest with you, I would like to keep it that way. Thank you so much for respecting my request," I said to him. "You're welcome gorgeous," he replied. There was an awkward silence, and I picked up the menu. "Go ahead and order what you would like, only the best for the best," he said.

"Heyyyyy," I thought to myself, and ordered one of the most expensive items on the menu. "Pastor, do you mind if I get a glass of wine?" I asked. "Why would I mind if you get some wine? You sitting up in here with your titties out enticing a brother, and then you got the nerve to ask me about drinking some wine? Who am I to tell you what you can and can't do?" he said, while laughing.

"Well you know, certain Pastors feel certain ways about different things, and I just wanted to make sure that I don't offend you," I replied. "Like I told you previously, only the best for the best. Go ahead and order the best wine on the menu," he said. "You won't have to tell me a third time," I said, as I ordered a meal with some expensive wine. He ordered an expensive meal as well. We laughed and talked as if we were old friends while we were waiting for our food to come.

The waitress came and asked us if there was anything else we needed when she bought our food. We both ordered two more glasses of wine, and dined sumptuously. "I know we've talked personally Pastor, but I want to go ahead and get back to the professional aspect of everything," I reminded him.

"So basically, I will be flying you down here 2x times a month. Each time you come, I will put you in a hotel, rent you a car, and pay you $2,000. It will be a total of $4,000 a month that you will be getting paid, and all of the expenses will be taken care of by the church. The only thing that I ask of you is to help motivate the women who attend services, and set them on fire for the Lord again," he said convincingly.

"Wow Pastor, that's very generous of you, and quite frankly, an offer I can't refuse," I said humbly. "You told me before that you worked hard to get to where you are, and it's just a blessing for us to have you. I want to make sure that you are compensated well above and beyond your worth," he said.

"If you're finished with dinner, let's go ahead and get out of here," he said. It looks like you've had a little bit too much to drink, and I don't want you getting back to your room too late," he said, in a concerned tone. "Wow, you're a true gentleman. Thank you for considering me and my safety," I said, feeling flattered. "No problem. As brothers and sisters in Christ, we always have to look out for each other," he said, as he pulled out his credit card, and put it in the billfold to pay.

The waiter came and took his card for payment. She came back about five minutes later and told him that his card was declined. I started to wonder, *how this man was going to pay me $4,000 a month, when he can't take care of this $350 bill for dinner.* "Oh, don't worry about this," he said, as I was looking at him crazy in the face. He pulled out another card, and gave it to the waiter.

"Periodically, my credit card company will put a block on my card, especially if it's for a purchase that's higher than normal. I'm sure that's the case," he said, trying to justify the BS that just went down." Yes, I understand. That has happened to me a time or two as well," I replied, while trying to make some light of the embarrassment his face was showing he was feeling.

"Yes, it is not fun. I wouldn't want you to have to wash the dishes tonight," he said, as we both laughed. I personally didn't find none of this shit funny, but tried to downplay it. "Sir, this card was declined as well," the waiter whispered in his ear. "How can that be?" he asked the waitress, as she stood there looking at him like he was crazy. "Give me a minute Ma'am. Let me call my credit card company," he said, while pulling out his cell phone.

As he dialed the number and put his card information in the automated system, I heard the automated system say that he had a $200 limit, and his balance was $275. *Oh hell naw! I'm in love with a man with a secured card*, I thought to myself. "They said that the hold time is over 20 minutes, and I'm not waiting that long," he said, as I heard a representative on the other line saying hello repeatedly before he hung up.

"Here, try this one," he said confidently, while handing a 3rd card to the waitress. I couldn't continue to be a part of the foolery, so I interjected. "Oh don't worry about it. I'll go ahead and take care of this one, and you can just reimburse me the 1st time you pay me. Does that sound good?" I asked him, as I gave my card to the waitress. "Yes it does, and I'm so sorry for this inconvenience. I'm so embarrassed," he said. "Don't be. Things happen. Trust me, I understand. I still want my money back," I said playfully, but I was dead ass serious.

"Girl, you're going to get your money, and then some, if you want it," he said winking. When the waiter came back, she gave me my credit card, and I signed the receipt. "Will you be able to leave the tip?" I asked sarcastically. He pulled his wallet out and put $20 on the table as if he was doing big things. I felt like it would be a slap in the face to tip her $20 on a $350 bill, so I left her a $75 tip on the card.

We got up to leave, and as we were walking out, a couple was walking in. "Pastor Tucker, it's so good to see you," the man said, looking at me as if he was confused. The couple, who I assumed to be husband and wife, was looking at him, and then looking at me, and then looking back at him. "Brother and Sister Leonard, how are y'all doing tonight?" he asked. "We are doing good," Sister Leonard said with a puzzled look on her face.

"I want to clear the air, and let y'all know that this isn't what it looks like. This is Yoshi Bowens, and I've hired her to do some work with our ladies in the church," he said reassuringly. "Don't you think that it would have been more appropriate for Sister Tucker to be here as well, so that when we see our Pastor out with a 'strange' woman, we don't have to jump to conclusions," she said, as she was looking me up and down.

"Quite frankly honey, that has nothing to do with you," Brother Leonard said to his wife sternly. "Yeah ok whatever," she said. She started walking away, but pulled her phone out, turned around, and took a picture of me and Pastor Tucker together. "I don't know what you are planning to do with that picture, but this is definitely not what it looks like. I have been hired by Pastor Tucker to do some work in the congregation, and can assure you that this is just simply business," I said, in a defensive manner. "Yeah whatever," Sister Leonard said, as she stomped away.

"Ummm, can I talk to you in private please?" Brother Leonard asked Brother Tucker. I stepped back some, but I was still close enough to hear what they were saying. "Brother Tucker, what are you doing here with her? You do know that everything about this is inappropriate right?" he asked Brother Tucker. "I'm not doing anything wrong though," he responded to Brother Leonard. "Does First Lady know that you're here with her?" Brother Leonard asked sarcastically. "Actually, she doesn't," Brother Tucker responded.

"I can't believe you'd put yourself back in this situation. It hasn't been too long ago since that other mess, and to be honest with you, people are still talking about it. Why would you go and do something like this again? I mean, look at that woman. She looks like a whole entree, and I know you're ready to eat," he said to Pastor Tucker. "It's not what it looks like man. Please believe me," Pastor Tucker said reassuringly.

"Well, I just want to thank you in advance for ruining my night, because this is all my wife is going to be talking about," Bro Leonard said in a disappointed tone. "Please reassure her that it's not a big deal, and that I'm not doing anything wrong. Trust me," he said, as he started walking away from him and out the door towards me.

"Wow, what was that all about?" I asked, as we were walking out. "Well, I am the leader of a church, and you're not my wife, so people start to assume things," he said, as if he was annoyed. "I heard him say people are still talking about something that happened before. What was he talking about?" I asked. "It's just 'he said, she said stuff.' I'm innocent until proven guilty, and I haven't been proven guilty," he responded sarcastically. "That's all I'm going to say about that, and you won't be asking me anything else about it either," he said, as he opened the door to my rental car.

"What hotel are you staying in? I'll follow you there to make sure you get there safely," he said.

"At the Glitzy Charleston on Grand street. Like you said, only the best for the best," I replied arrogantly. "I'm right behind you," he said. As I was driving, my heart was pounding. I knew if he came up to my room, I was gonna be riding Pastor's dick tonight.

We pulled up to the hotel, and I motioned for him to pull on the side of me. "They have security in the parking lot, so I'll be fine from here," I told him. "Are you sure? I don't mind walking you up to your room," he said convincingly. "I'm a big girl, I'll be just fine. Besides, I'm really exhausted, and I just want to go to bed," I responded. "I think you should let me tuck you in," he said seductively. My inner hoe said 'come on up,' but the rational part of me said, "The spirit is willing, but the flesh is weak Pastor," and I pulled off like a boss.

I parked my car in the parking lot, and stopped by the hotel bar to get another drink. I sat there drinking for about 10 minutes, and drunkenly walked into the hotel's elevator. The elevator stopped at the eleventh floor, and I stumbled to my room. I put my head down to get the room key out of my purse, and as soon as I looked up, I looked right into Pastor Tucker's face.

"So, we meet again huh?" Pastor Tucker asked me. "What are you doing here?" I asked, in a surprised tone. "Calm down already, I just needed to use the bathroom, and the bathroom downstairs in the lobby is out of order. I mean, a brother is good enough to come in to use the bathroom, isn't he?"

"You are, but I am kindly asking for you to leave after you use the bathroom. This very innocent situation can be taken out of context if seen by the wrong person, and per what the man we just left said, you don't need any additional mess in your life," I said sternly. "Will do," he reassured me, after walking behind me into my room.

He walked into the bathroom, and I sat down on the bed, took my shoes off, and put on my sexy, short robe to get a little more comfortable. He came out of the bathroom fully undressed, with his penis rock hard. The look on my face must've been saying something, as he said, "I'm just offering you what you don't have the courage to ask for."

"I apologize if I gave you the wrong impression, but this is not cool. I want you to leave my room right now!" I yelled at him. "And I want you to suck my dick right now," he said, walking towards me with his penis standing at attention, looking like a meal. He started rubbing the head of his dick all over my face and mouth. My inner hoe couldn't help but pull it in my mouth, and start licking and sucking on it like it was a big piece of pork sausage, and I LOVE pork sausages.

He moaned and groaned as if it was the best head he ever had. He then took his big strong hands, and started to massage my pussy. He used my juices to stick his fingers in and out of me, while I continued to satisfy him with my mouth. He pushed me back on the bed, opened my legs, and went to stick his dick in me. "Do you have a condom?" I asked him. "No, I don't just walk around with condoms on me," he replied sarcastically.

"Just shut up, and take this dick," he whispered in my ear. And that's exactly what I did, shut up, and took that dick. He pumped steadily in and out for a good 5 minutes, before he blasted off up in me. His moans and groans sounded heavenly, but I was so disappointed with the 5 minutes he gave me.

He laid down in the bed when I rolled over on the top of him, and started kissing him in the mouth. He quickly turned his head in disgust, and said, "Don't kiss me, I don't know where ya mouth has been," in a serious tone. "That didn't matter a minute ago when it was on your dick, now did it?" I responded sarcastically.

I then went to hug on him when he said, "Nah, we ain't doing that either. What we did was what it was. Please don't try to make it more than that," he said arrogantly, as he sat up from the bed and started putting his clothes on. His phone rang, and he went into the bathroom to answer it.

"Hey babe, yes, I remember it's your birthday. The deacons meeting went a little longer than I expected. I'm going to stop and pick up a cake for you, and then I'll be home. I love you too," he responded. He came out of the bathroom, and I was playing on my phone as if I hadn't heard his whole conversation. He headed towards the door. "I'll be in contact with you," he said, as he walked out of my room.

Tears started rolling down my face, and I felt like a big fool. He played me, and had me feeling like something I hadn't felt in years, a straight up hoe. Ever since the day I laid eyes on him, I'd envisioned how this would play out, but I'd never imagined that it would've been like this. I couldn't help but call him. The phone rang a few times, and then he sent me to voicemail.

I thought about how I jeopardized my self-worth, my life, and my marriage over 5 minutes, and they weren't even 5 good minutes. I mean, I didn't nut or nothing.

I sat up and listened to him lie to his wife about who he was on the phone with. I then heard him lie to me about who he was talking to on the other line when he thought he clicked over. He then lied at the dinner table about being on hold with the bank, when I heard the representative on the other line. A member of his church called him out for being in a mess with another woman.

What was I thinking of even getting into this mess? What did I think would be the end result? That he'd leave his wife and family for someone he doesn't even know? If he was so willing to step out on his wife with someone that he doesn't know, why do I even want him? This man couldn't even afford to pay for my dinner, yet, I let him stick his raw dick in my body.

My thoughts are all over the place, and I am heavy hearted. I legit just got played, not by my own husband, but by someone else's husband. I hate his dog ass right now, but is he really to blame? *He only did what I allowed him to do. This can't be life, and I'm way too old and wise to be indulged in this foolishness.*

I'm so disappointed in myself! I feel like I just want to hide under a rock, and never come out again, is all I could think to myself. Crying myself to sleep has become my new normal, and tonight is no exception to my new normal. I cried until I felt like I couldn't cry any longer.

Chapter 13

THE DAY OF the conference, I woke up heavy-hearted, and I felt ashamed of myself. To add insult to injury, his wife will be the first person that I see while I'm speaking, as she has a front row ticket. Everything in me wants to just cancel this engagement, but I've worked very hard building my brand to get to this point. If I cancel, I will be losing a lot of money, as I won't get paid. I needed to get my mind right in order to motivate a room of over 1000 women, and how else do I do that? I go to my Father in prayer.

"Dear Lord,

I am wrong. What I did, and who I did it with was wrong. I have dishonored myself, my family, and most importantly, You. I have sinned, and I am repenting for those sins. Lord, please don't allow my sins to find me out. Please allow this situation to go away, without any repercussions or consequences. Please give me the strength to never deal with him again.

In the name of Jesus,

I pray,"

Amen

After my prayer, I felt a little better. I showered and got myself together, hopped in the car, and headed to the event. I arrived early, and went into the venue so that I could set up for the event.

My phone vibrated, and it was a video message. "We love you Mommy, you are the best Mommy ever," the three little voices said in the video. The phone buzzed again, and it was a video from Leon. "I've been thinking since our last conversation, and I want to work on us. When you come home, we're going to get back to us, the way we used to be. I love you girl," he said, with a big smile.

I started crying so hard. I forgot all about my family when I made that selfish decision last night. *What type of wife and mother am I?* is all I could think to myself. I became so overwhelmed with guilt, and I started to feel so defeated. I sat down with tears rolling down my face, when someone came up behind me and tapped me on my shoulder.

"Sis, are you okay?" a warm and friendly voice asked me. I looked up with my makeup smeared all over my face, and looked right into Sister Tucker's face. My heart started pounding, and I was at a loss for words. "Oh hey sis, I'm okay. I'm just a little overwhelmed with emotion right now. I've worked so hard to have gotten to this point, and I'm finally here. My dreams have manifested and come into fruition," I lied convincingly.

"I was thinking about that, and then I just got a video message from my husband and kids which made me even more emotional than I already was," I said. "I definitely understand. My husband does the same thing to me before I do something big as well, so I completely understand your emotions," she replied.

"I didn't sleep well last night, so I decided to come here early. Please don't allow me to disrupt you while you're preparing for your engagement. I'll just be back here getting some sleep," she said. "Oh really? You didn't sleep well last night?" I asked inquisitively. "Girl, I got a lot going on, but nothing that's too hard for God," she said, as she walked away. Looking into her eyes after knowing what I've done, made me feel a thousand times worse than I was already feeling. A cloud of regret shadowed over me, and I just wished I could turn back the hands of time.

Chapter 14

"WHY DO WE keep finding ourselves in this compromising position? We are both dead wrong for being here," Kat reminded Leon. "Don't mess up the moment baby. We both are where we want to be right now with no regrets, aren't we?" he asked, as he sat up straight in the bed. "Yes, this is what I want, but I just feel so bad about it. I mean, I know that you're a married man, and if I was a married woman, I wouldn't want another woman to do this with my husband," she said.

"You're not doing anything wrong. Legally, me and Yoshi are married. In real life, we're just roommates. As soon as me and Yoshi get divorced, I'm going to marry you, and we're going to live happily ever after," he told Kat with a big smile.

"We're going to have babies, you're not going to have to work anymore, and I'm going to buy you everything your heart desires. Doesn't that sound good to you? I'm a man of my word," he said reassuringly. "I mean, that sounds good Leon, but we both know that's not how life really works. I mean, even the Bible says you will reap what you sow, doesn't it, man of God?" she asked sarcastically.

"Yes it does say that, but it also says that God is merciful and just enough to forgive us. Now shut up, and put this dick in ya mouth," he said sarcastically. "Yes Pastor," she replied, as she made his wish her command. As she passionately made love to his manhood with her mouth, he moaned and groaned.

"Get off of it, I want to get in that pussy," he said. She stopped sucking it, and turned over flat on her back. "That's why I love you so much. You always do exactly what Pastor tells you to do," he said. As soon as she laid down, he put her legs up in the air and passionately made love to her. He started moaning, groaning, and screaming while stroking faster. "God is good," he yelled, while ejaculating inside of Kat.

He got from off the top of her, and laid down beside her in the bed. "Girl, if I never told you before that I love you, I'm telling you now. I love you," he said, with a serious look, holding her face between the palms of his hands. "I love you too Pastor," she said, in a soft voice. "After all that big, good dick I just served you, I can't get a little bit more excitement out of you?" he asked sarcastically.

"I'm so sorry. I enjoyed it, but I just feel so bad for what we've done to your wife, and we've done it so irresponsibly. We ain't use no protection, and you just laid up here and nutted in me," she said to Leon. "You act like this is the 1st time we've gotten down like this. The 1st time you were all for it. Now you have a conscious?" he asked, sounding confused.

"What about if I get pregnant? I'm not on the pill or nothing, and it'll just be my luck that I will get pregnant just because of the sinful circumstances behind our actions," Kat said. "If you get pregnant, it will be the Lord's will. Babies are a blessing from the Lord himself. We'll handle it like good Christian parents, and raise our baby in the nurture and admonition of the Lord," he said, in a reassuring manner.

"And then there's STD'S. I mean, you don't look like you got a disease, but hell these days, you can't tell just by looking at people," she said concerningly. "Wow, it's really like that? Now you going to sit up here and try to offend me talking about I don't look like I got no disease, when you just allowed me to do what you wanted me to do to you? Seriously, how does that make you look and sound as a woman?" he yelled at her.

"You got some nerve," he said, as he got up out of her bed, and started putting his clothes on. "Where are you going?" she asked sadly. "Don't worry about where I'm going. As a matter of fact, I'll go to the clinic and get some antibiotics since I got a disease," he said sarcastically. "I didn't mean it like that," she said sadly. "Naw you're right, I probably do have a disease being that I've slept with your nasty desperate ass. I can name 5 men that been up in you, and several of them are members of the church," he responded angrily.

"Wowwww. I'm being honest with you about what was done, and what can happen as a consequence of what was done, and you gonna disrespect and leave me like I'm some slut on the street?" she yelled to him. "Isn't that where I initially found you, on the street?" he asked her, as he walked out of the room to leave her house.

"I don't expect to hear from you again," he said sternly, just before slamming her front door and leaving her house. Kat ran out of the room and watched him leave from her front room window. His clothes were sloppy, and he looked like he just got finished doing what he did. As he was walking down the porch stairs, the mailman walked up.

"Pastor Bowens, it's so good to see you man," he said excitedly. Caught off guard and stuttering, Pastor replied, "Deacon Johnson, it's good to see you as well. Please excuse me, I have to get to a meeting," Pastor Leon said, as he was stopped in his tracks when Brother Johnson reached out to shake his hand.

"I take it Sister Bowens is in there as well Pastor?" Brother Johnson said, as he nodded his head towards her house with one eyebrow raised in suspicion. "Yoshi's birthday is coming up, and we are planning a surprise party for her," he said, as he was stumbling over his words, trying not to look or act guilty.

"Please forgive me if I'm out of line Pastor, but you are looking a little 'guilty of something,' he said, looking at Pastor's unloosened belt. The woman that lives here is finnnneee," he said, putting an emphasis on fine. "I can't help but think that you were there for the wrong reason

Pastor. I mean, you are a man of the cloth, but you're still a man, and that woman in there is just simply irresistible," Brother Johnson said to Pastor. "I think Jesus would have been tempted to hit that too," Brother Johnson said, laughing hysterically.

"And just to let you know Pastor, between me and you, it is as good as it looks," he said. "Awww man, that's just too much information. There are some things that your Pastor just does not need to know my brother," Leon said. "My bad man, look I'm sorry again for getting the wrong impression about you and her. I know that you're a man of good report and reputation, heck, you are my spiritual leader. Please forgive me for thinking the worst of you," he said, as he extended his hand again to shake Leon's hand.

"No, I appreciate you speaking on it. The Bible states that if you see your brother in sin that you should go to him, and to him alone to try and have him restored. I appreciate you looking out for my soul brother," Leon said. "Anytime. You know we have to look out for each other," Brother Johnson said proudly.

Leon started to walk towards his car when he turned back towards Brother Johnson and said, "There's one more thing. Please don't tell anyone that you saw me here. Again, it's a surprise birthday party for Yoshi, and invitations aren't open to everyone in the church. It's a small gathering for her friends and loved ones, so I don't need this to get back to the church," Leon told Brother Johnson.

"Only under one circumstance," Brother Johnson said. "What's that?" Leon asked, looking confused. "Can a brother get an invitation?" he asked Leon. "Most definitely," Leon replied, as he got into his car. Leon slammed his head back into the headrest, and thought about how irresponsible It was for him to even get into this situation, and then to be caught leaving her house.

He knew it was a bad situation, and had a feeling that it wasn't going to end well. *What in the world have I gotten myself into*, he thought to himself, while pulling off. Kat closed the blinds after Leon pulled off and Brother Johnson delivered her mail. She busted out crying and started praying.

"Dear Lord,

Please forgive me for I have sinned. I have done wrong, and I kindly ask that You please forgive me for my sins. Please bless me with my own man so that I don't have to sneak around with another woman's man. I feel worthless and cheap right now Lord, and I'm so sorry. Please help me not to have any negative consequences from this situation, and please help me not to do this again in the future.

In the name of Jesus,

I pray,

Amen."

Chapter 15

KAT FELT A little better after the prayer, and went to lay down. After about 5 minutes, she dozed off, when she was rudely interrupted by loud knocks on her door. She went and answered the door, and there was the postman looking at a woman who was naked up under her sexy robe.

"Oh hey there. Do you have a package for me to sign or something? What brings you here?" she asked, slightly annoyed. "No, I was just delivering your mail, and I wanted to check to see if you were okay," he replied, in a concerned tone. "Why wouldn't I be okay? I'm just fine," she said. "Well you sure are looking good," he said, as he was staring at her hard nipples through her silk robe.

"Thank you, but again, how is it that I can help you?" she asked embarrassingly. "Well, something weird happened," he admitted. "Something weird?" she asked him, looking confused. "Yes, something really weird. As I was doing my route, I saw Pastor coming out of your house. He was looking upset, and acting hastily. Now, you do realize that the Pastor that just came out of your house is the leader of our church, and a married man, right?" he asked sarcastically.

"And your point?" she replied, with mad attitude. "My point is that you are a young, single, fine woman standing at the door fully naked up under that robe, but yet he left out of here not even 10 minutes ago. I mean, even I have hit it a few times, so I know how you roll," he replied bluntly. "So now you fucking Pastor?" he asked angrily.

"How dare you accuse me of such a thing? I happen to love and respect Pastor and First Lady as my spiritual Mother and Father. I would never degrade myself, or sin against God like that," she said, in an upset manner. "Oh, so you mean to tell me that if your earthly Father came to visit you, you'd be naked up under your robe?" he asked her. "For your information, I was fully clothed when he left, and then I put my robe on to get more comfortable, because I was by myself. What is the problem with that?" she yelled loudly.

"Umm hmm," he said, as he was nodding his head up and down sarcastically. "So, what was he here for then?" he asked her. "First of all, I owe you no explanations. The last time I checked, I pay rent up in here. Until that changes, I don't have to answer to you or nobody else," she said, while rolling her eyes.

"Why are you getting so defensive? You're acting like you're guilty to me," he said to her. "You sound like a man that is overstepping his boundaries to me. Who do you think you are?" she asked angrily. "I'm a man that just saw something that I know that y'all didn't want me to see, but I saw it anyhow. Pastor is rushing out of your house, you come to the door with a robe on wit ya nipples hard as a rock. That only means one thing to me, Y'ALL FUCKIN," he said, nodding his head with confidence.

"Please go. I'm not going to allow you and your false accusations to ruin my day," she said, in an aggravated tone. "Oh, I'm not going nowhere," he said, as he started laughing while pushing her into the house. "What are you doing?" she asked, in a scared tone. "I'm about to get done to me what Pastor just had done to him," he said slyly, while rubbing his hands together. "Well grab your Bible then, because that's all that happened. We had a Bible study," she said sarcastically.

"Oh yeah, let me ask you a question. What day is the party on?" he asked her. "What are you talking about now?" she asked, with an attitude. "Pastor told me that y'all was in here planning a party. What day is it?" he asked inquisitively.

"Well it's not a party. It's the Appreciation Day for Pastor that we were talking about," she said nervously, making it obvious that she was lying, and coming up with things to say as she continued talking.

"Appreciation Day? Yeah, so what day is the appreciation going to be on?" he asked. "We haven't got a date set in stone yet, so we were just speaking about some preliminary things," she said. "Don't you think that his wife needed to be a part of that conversation? As a matter of fact, don't you think that it would have been more appropriate if this conversation would have taken place at the church with the deacons and other members, versus in your home, in the middle of the day?

The last time I checked, your name isn't on any type of advisory board for anything," he reminded her. "We were just brainstorming. You're reading way more into this than what it is," she replied, in a frustrated tone. "So what about the other party," he asked her? "What party are you talking about now? I'm confused," she said.

"The party for Yoshi. I mean, Pastor told me that y'all was in here planning a party for Yoshi, and now you tell me that y'all was brainstorming ideas for his appreciation day. I'm just trying to figure out which lie is true at this point," he said sarcastically.

"Oh yeah, he did mention that he wanted to throw her a party for some award she just won, and for being a Speaker for the Essential Conference. It's kind of like a congratulatory celebration. She's worked so hard, and I'm so proud of all of her wins," she said boldly.

"So that's how you show her that you're proud of her, by fucking her husband? You trifling bitch," he yelled at her. "Oh, and by the way, Pastor told me y'all was working on a surprise party for Yoshi.

I guess he forgot that her birthday was six months ago, and that he had me deliver flowers to her on her birthday. So, I've concluded that both of y'all are lying, which just further proves my original theory of the fact that y'all fuckin," he said confidently.

"Get out of my house right now! I want you out of here," she screamed at him. "No, I'm not going nowhere. Not until after you suck my dick. Oh, and this time, it ain't gonna be none of that 'spitting the nut out,' you gon swallow ALL this nut," he said, as he sat down and unbuckled his belt to pull his meat out.

"I stopped this with you before because my conscience was bothering me too bad. You are a married man, and I don't want to get back into this with you. I happen to love your wife, and she's a really good person. I can't do this with you now or ever again," she said to him. "Oh yeah, since when did you stop sleeping with married men? After Pastor left out of here?" he asked her. She bowed her head in shame, and started to cry. "Please don't make me do this with you, I'm begging you," she pleaded.

"I'm going to put it like this. Your secret is safe with me, but only if I get what I want, whenever I want it, and I've just told you what I want. And I want it NOW! Or, shall I take this news back to the Saints?" he asked, in a slick tone. "They'll never believe you. It'll be your word against mine, and the way you did your wife with that other woman, you won't stand a chance. Your word means nothing to the Saints, as you've already discredited yourself, and showed them you were nothing but a liar and cheater when you got caught," she said confidently.

"Oh, ye of little faith," he said, while laughing. "If that situation that your bringing up has taught me nothing else, it's always taught me to be pinpoint accurate. As a result, I keep this," he said, as he pulled a little device from off his vest.

"And what is that?" she asked sarcastically. "It's a camera. All I have to do is press play, and it will show where Pastor came out of the house with his belt unbuckled looking like a chicken with his head cut off. Now if that ocular proof isn't enough evidence for the Saints, I don't know what is," he snapped back at her.

"So once again, I want you to remind me of how you do what it is that you do. I miss it," he said, as he untied her robe while looking at her smooth brown body. "I hate you, I really do!" she yelled at him while crying. "I hope you didn't let him fuck you in the ass, did you? You know you promised me that was just for me and you right?" he asked while laughing.

She came close to him, got down on the floor in between his knees, pulled his meat out, and did what he asked her to do. As she was sucking it, he told her to get off it. He got on top of her, started kissing her passionately, stuck his dick inside of her, and nutted in her. He got from off the top of her, and went into the bathroom to take a shower. He came back out, got dressed and took some money out of his wallet. "Thanks for the good time. When you act like a hoe, you get treated like a hoe," he said, as he threw a dollar in her face, before walking out of the door.

Chapter 16

Y A GIRL GOT a standing ovation at the conference today. I did my thang. I talked about self-esteem, motivation, money, and men. The ladies and I had a really good time today. There were a lot of laughs, some tears, and some very empowering moments. I got a standing ovation from the ladies, and sold hundreds of copies of my book.

Sister Tucker sat right in the first row, so I'd see her very often while I was speaking. She seemed to really be enjoying herself, and I saw her laughing at different times. That made me feel really good, as I feel bad for contributing to her pain, even if she doesn't know about it.

When the conference was over, I hurried to the bathroom, as I had been holding my pee the whole time I was speaking. I heard someone else walk in the bathroom and put their items on the bathroom counter.

As I was finishing up, I heard a loud sob. A woman started crying so loudly, I was skeptical about leaving the stall, as I didn't know what was going on out there.

I finished up and flushed the toilet. As I was walking out of the stall, I saw Sister Tucker bent over the bathroom sink with her face in her hands crying. After I washed my hands, I ran up to her, grabbed her, and hugged her.

"Oh my gosh, Sister Tucker, what's wrong? Is everything OK?" I asked frantically. She looked over at me and quickly wiped her eyes. "Yes, I just have a lot going on," she said sadly. "I can understand that," I replied. I grabbed her hands, and started to pray with her.

"Heavenly Father,

I come to You on behalf of my sister in Christ. She is burdened down and heavy hearted. I don't know what the situation is, but You do Lord. Please soothe her mind, and put peace in her heart. Please help her to remember that there is nothing that she, her husband, and You can't handle.

As soon as I mentioned her husband, she started sobbing even more. I stopped praying, let her hands go, and ran and got some paper towels for her. I gave her the paper towels so she could blow her nose and wipe her tears. I took her hands again so that we could continue the prayer. Please Lord, help her to remember that there is nothing too hard for You. Lord, please show up and show out in this circumstance, and please help her and Pastor to stay strong while enduring the trials that they face.

In the name of Jesus,

I pray,

Amen,"

After the prayer, I just stood there looking at her. I grabbed her and hugged her. I wanted to apologize to her for being one of the reasons why she is in pain, but I couldn't bring myself to do it. As I looked at her and saw the hurt in her eyes, again, I felt like the most horrible person in the world.

"My gosh, I feel like a weight has been lifted off of me," she stated. "Well I'm so glad, because we can't run this race loaded down," I replied. The inquisitive part of me wanted to know what was going on with 'our man,' and if she knew about what happened last night with me and her husband. I just know that this woman would beat my ass in this bathroom if she knew that I was with her husband last night.

There was this long awkward silence that I broke by saying, "If you want to talk about what's going on, I'm here. Please know that you have a friend in me," I said, in a reassuring tone. "Oh yeah? Do I really have a friend in you?" she asked sarcastically. At this point, my heart is ready to come out of my chest, because I now know that she knows. *How am I going to get myself out of this situation? What can I possibly say to this woman whose heart is broken into pieces because of what I did?* I thought to myself.

I wanted to let her know that I didn't mean for it to happen. *I mean, one thing led to another, and it just happened. I feel like I need to be a woman about mine, and confess. I mean, if she asked me about being with him, how would I respond? Am I gonna say that I wasn't with him, or that I didn't do anything with him? I mean, we got caught together at the restaurant, hell that bitch took a picture of me with him.* I had so many thoughts running through my mind at this moment, and I was confused, speechless, and at a loss for words.

"You have been in my life for less than a week, and because of you, my life is now changed forever. When I first met you, I knew that you would have a big impact on my life, but I never knew that it would be in this manner," she said angrily.

I opened my mouth to start explaining my side of the story, when she put her finger up and said, "I'm talking, you can speak when I'm finished." Now, had I not been with her husband last night, I woulda went off on her for being disrespectful. *Who in the hell does she think she's talking to?* is all I could think to myself. I then snapped back to reality, and realized that I could give her this moment respectfully, the same way her husband gave me a moment last night.

"Let me ask you a few questions," she said, as she got up close to me in my face. I balled my fists up just in case I needed to knock her out. Yes, I was wrong, but I'm gonna always defend myself. "Has your husband ever cheated on you? If your husband did cheat on you, did he cheat on you with someone that you knew and respected?" she asked. I opened my mouth to answer, but she interrupted me.

"How would you feel if you knew the woman that your husband cheated on you with? I mean, this is a woman who told you that you had a friend in her. This is a woman who prayed with you during a bad time in your life. Then you find out that she is the very woman that your husband cheated on you with. Again, how would you feel?" she asked, in a very serious tone.

I didn't respond immediately, because I had gotten used to her telling me to stop talking. "You can talk now," she said sarcastically. "Thank you for allowing me to speak my sister. I would feel very hurt and betrayed," I replied sadly. "With that being said, I want to say something to you," she said. At that moment, I made up my mind to be a grown woman about the situation, and apologize. "I'm sorry that I sle…," I started to say. I couldn't even get the sentence out good before she started screaming. "You're sorry, you're sorry?" she yelled. At this point, I knew that shit was about to hit the fan.

All I could visualize in my head is me going viral on social media for getting dragged across the floor. The caption would say something along the lines of, "Married motivational speaker gets dragged by preacher's wife for doing exactly what she tells other women not to do, and that's sleep with someone else's man."

"You got the nerve to be sorry? You come into my life, and because of you, things are gonna be different forever. My life will never be the same again. My relationship status with my husband will change forever. Has anyone ever called you a homewrecker before?" she asked.

At this point, I'm just straight up sad. I felt the big lump in my throat that I always feel before I'm about to cry, and I started shaking. *You need to calm down and hold your composure*, I thought to myself. I said a quick prayer to myself.

"Dear Lord,

I know I'm wrong, but please don't fail me now.

In the name of Jesus,

I pray,

Amen."

I broke the long awkward silence by saying, "No. I have never been called a homewrecker before, and I sincerely apologize to you for wrecking your home, if that's what I've done. That definitely wasn't my intent, and I pray that you'll find it in your heart to forgive me," I said, with tears rolling down my face.

"Forgive you, you want me to forgive you after what you've done to me?" she asked, while laughing. She got all up in my personal space, and as she talked, I could smell her breath. I then understood why Pastor cheated on her with me. *This girl's breath is horrible*, I thought to myself, as I chuckled on the inside.

"See in a situation like this, what's done is done," she said. I looked at her in confusion, as her range of emotions caused my life to flash right before my eyes. "You have no need to apologize to me, because you've done no wrong to me. There's nothing for me to forgive you for, and there's nothing that you've done wrong to me. As a matter of fact, you did everything right," she told me.

"I did?" I replied, feeling confused. "You see, you stood up and talked to a group of women, and you kept it real with us. You personally spoke to my brokenness, and reminded me that I shouldn't be settling or dealing with any of the mess that I've been putting up with in my marriage. You reminded me that I need to love me more than I love him. I thank you for that sis," she said in a sincere tone, while grabbing my hands.

"You're welcome," I responded, feeling relieved. "Finally, the Lord has answered my prayers. To be honest sis, I've been struggling with my Christianity, as it feels like my prayers are falling on deaf ears. I've been praying for years to have a baby, and I haven't been able to conceive.

Treatment after treatment, and nothing's happening. On top of my fertility issues, he's been cheating on me. As a result, I've been contemplating getting a divorce," she told me.

"Just last week, I got a call from my GYN doctor. She told me she had some important news to tell me. I called off work, and went straight to the store to set up a baby registry, because I just knew she'd be giving me the news I've been waiting for. My gynecologist sat down with me, held my hands, and told me that she had some good news and bad news, and asked me which news I wanted to hear first," Sister Tucker told me. I was all ears as Sister Tucker was talking. "Oh my sis, what did she say? I asked. "Well, it's kind of personal, but I know that I can trust you. She told me the bad news first, and I now know that at this point of time, I have herpes, gonorrhea, and chlamydia," she said sadly.

"That was the bad news? Well hell, what was the good news?" I blurted out unexpectedly. "The good news is that at this point, I don't have full blown AIDS, but I have contracted HIV from my husband. "Oh my goodness sis, this is deep," I replied. "Yep, this is the price that I've paid for being virtuous and loving to my husband. For 6 years, I haven't looked at another man sexually or in a lustful way. I've been nothing but faithful to my husband, and this is the thanks I get?" she asked me.

"You do things the right way, and things still come out messed up. He's the only man that I've ever been with sexually, and I'm devastated. The doctor even told me that my fertility issues may be a result of the STD's. Gonorrhea and chlamydia are able to be treated, but the HIV and herpes are something that I have to live with for the rest of my life," she said, as we both stood there crying. "I'm mad, I'm mad as hell. Excuse me sis," she said, as she ran into a bathroom stall crying her eyes out.

She cried and cried in that stall, and I cried and cried outside the stall. No one, and I mean no one should have to endure the type of pain she's enduring. I stood there waiting for her to come out and when she did, she looked better. "I'm so sorry to lay all this on you sis. It's just that I've been praying to God to send me someone that I can trust, and then you pop up in my life. I truly believe that you are that person. I feel that you are the answer to my prayers," she said sincerely.

"Oh, and I forgot to tell you. My gynecologist just happens to be a member of the church. She also has a sister and a best friend that goes there as well, so I know that they all know this about me. Can you imagine what's being said about me and my husband? On top of that, he doesn't even know that I know. As a matter of fact, I'm not sure if he knows his own health status, as he never goes to the doctor," she admitted. "Can my life get any worse at this point?" she asked, while laughing. "Don't mind me, I have to laugh to keep from crying again," she said.

"Your current circumstances have truly made me sad," I admitted to her. "I'm so sorry that you're having to deal with all of this, especially all alone," I said, as I gave her a long hug. "I don't know why you're sad," she said. "After this is over, you'll go back home to your perfect life and your perfect family, and I'll be left here sick and withering away," she said sarcastically.

"My life is far from perfect sis, you don't even know the half," I told her. "Well, there is a bright side to all of this stuff," she said, as we backed away from each other after the hug. "The women that he's dealt with have the same diagnosis as me. They will have to deal with sores on their vagina. They will have to deal with nasty vaginal smells and funny colored discharge. They now have the HIV virus in their system, and I take pleasure in knowing that I won't be suffering alone.

I'm so happy that there is at least one other woman out there with me that knows or will be finding out about her multiple diagnosis. Karma is truly a bitch, isn't it?" she asked me, as if she knew I was one of the women he'd dealt with.

My stomach started turning, and I started feeling sick due to the revelation. "Sis, I hate to leave you here, but I need to get going to the airport to make sure that I catch my flight on time. I will definitely be praying for you, and I'll remain in contact with you. We'll get through this together," I said, as I reached to give her another hug. "Here's my number," I said to her, as I handed her another business card.

"That won't be necessary. I found your business card in my husband's pocket this morning. I went to wash his clothes after he fell asleep this morning. He failed to come home last night, which just happened to be my birthday. I ended up spending my birthday alone," she admitted.

My heart started pounding again, as I was trying to think of what to say now.

"You're right sis, I did give him my business card on Sunday, as he said he may want to hire me to speak at the ladies day program you all will be having," I replied quickly. "Right, we would love to have you come speak for us," she said, as we started to walk out of the bathroom. "Thanks again for the motivation. I appreciate you," she said, as she grabbed and hugged me again.

"It was my pleasure," I said, as I watched her disappear into the crowd. Perfect life huh? She has no idea how much more complicated my life has become since she's dropped this bombshell on me. *This seriously cannot be life for me right now,* is all I was thinking on the way to the airport.

I can't believe that what was supposed to be one of the happiest moments of my life, has actually turned out to be one of the worst moments of my life.

I've been told that I may have gonorrhea, chlamydia, herpes, and HIV. I have a broken heart. I broke my marriage vows, and I caused another sister pain, when she thinks she has a friend in me. Sins come at a price, and this price is just too expensive for some wack, infested, 5-minute dick. It definitely wasn't worth it, and I'm super disappointed in myself for the part I played in all of this, is all I've been thinking to myself.

I had to run through the airport to catch the plane, because I lost track of time while speaking with Sister Tucker. I boarded the plane, and immediately ordered three drinks. I wished that I could just drink my life away. I started crying, just thinking about what I'd done to Leon and the kids. Even though I'm not feeling Leon at this time, he didn't deserve what I did to him.

The worst thing about this is that all that will happen because of this, hasn't even happened yet. This weight is honestly too much for me to bear. Even though I'm halfway drunk, I still felt the need to pray.

"Dear Lord,

I have sinned against You. My actions will cause devastation and destruction to innocent people, and I am so sorry. I know I deserve everything that comes with my actions, but I humbly ask You to spare me from the consequences. Please allow this situation to be swept up under the rug so that I don't bring myself, my family, and most importantly the church, to an open shame.

In the name of Jesus,

I pray,"
Amen

Chapter 17

AFTER I PRAYED, I dozed off for the remainder of the flight. When the flight landed, I got my luggage and headed out to catch a cab. A familiar car pulled up with a handsome man in it. "Can I give you a ride beautiful?" the man yelled from the open window. I looked and saw that it was my husband, and a feeling of peace came over me. I ran to the car, and hugged him as if I've never hugged him before.

"So, how's my conference motivational speaker doing?" he asked excitedly. "I'm doing well, glad to be back home though," I said. "Well, tell me all about it. How come you don't seem excited about it?" he asked. "I am happy about it, I'm just not feeling well right now. I think it may have been something I ate," I lied. "Oh, my poor baby. As soon as we get home, I will run you a hot bath, wash your back for you, and put you to sleep, just like I used to do in the old days," he said, in a comforting tone.

"You don't know how good that sounds baby. I'm truly looking forward to it. It's been a long time, and I'm glad you're doing something that will help us get back to us. I miss you, I miss us," I replied enthusiastically. "Well, we have to start somewhere, and I figured this was the perfect way for us to get reunited. To be honest with you, I miss us too, and I'm 100% committed to doing what needs to be done to make this marriage work. I even dropped the kids off at your mom's so that we can have an uninterrupted moment together," he said charmingly.

"Wow, that sounds like music to my ears! You have no idea how much I needed to hear what you just said to me. It's so reassuring to know that you are wanting to make this work, just as much as I am, and that you do still love me," I said happily. We pulled up to the house, and he took my luggage in for me. He went straight to the bathroom, lit some candles, and ran me a hot bubble bath. I sat in the tub for over an hour, trying to soak and scrub the possible STDs away, but ended up getting out of the tub feeling even more dirty than I was before I got into the tub.

Leon was there to dry me off, and escorted me to the bed. He laid me down, opened up my legs, and started giving me some head. Just as I started to get into it, he stopped. "Damn babe, did you wash it?" he asked, in disgust. "Wash what?" I asked confusingly. "Ya pussy! It should be a sin for your pussy to be that stank. I can't believe that you'd have me eat your pussy while you are on your period," he yelled angrily.

"I'm not on my period bae. You know I would never do no nasty stuff like that," I replied defensively. "I also know that it's something that's seriously wrong with your pussy. You got to go get that checked out Bae. I smelled it when you initially got in the car, but figured it was due to sweat from your day of traveling. I don't know, maybe you got a bad yeast infection or something, but you definitely need to go get it checked out. As a matter of fact, I'll go with you," he said, in a commanding tone.

Once again, I'm in bed looking sick and feeling embarrassed. "I'm so sorry about this bae! I can't believe that I ruined such a good moment like this," I said sadly. "It's all good. Out of 12 years, I've never smelled it like this before, so I'll give you a pass for one stank day," he said, trying to make me feel better. "Well can I at least suck it?" I asked. "No! That smell has turned me off, but come here and lay in Daddy's arms so you and your stank pussy can go to sleep," he chuckled. I went to lay in his arms, and to my surprise, I got a text message notification.

"How come I haven't heard from you?" the text message from Pastor Tucker asked. "Who is that texting you at this time of night?" Leon asked. "The event coordinator," I quickly replied. "She wanted to make sure that I got in okay," I said convincingly. "Okay. Turn the phone off, and go to sleep," he demanded. "Yes sir," I replied. I got in his arms, but all I can think about is Pastor Tucker.

I called him several times since he left my room, and he's been sending me to voicemail, but now he wants to know why he hasn't heard from me? Why is he playing games with me?

Ever since I've talked with Sister Tucker, I'm even more upset with him. He left out of my room, but didn't go home. *Where the hell did he go and who the hell was he with?* I wondered to myself. As much as I wanted to hate him for what he could've possibly done to my life, deep down inside, I still yearn for him. I wanted to call him back, just so that I could hear his voice.

Even after the way he treated me, I must admit that I still have feelings for him, and I'm in love with him. I never thought that my life would be one in which me and my stank pussy are laid up with my husband fantasizing and thinking about another man. Lord, help me please...

Chapter 18

IT'S A BRAND-NEW day, and I woke up with Pastor Tucker on my mind. I called him, and after the second ring, he sent me to voicemail. I was feeling pretty good, but after being sent to voicemail yet again, I started feeling down. I definitely needed a pep talk, so who better to call than best friend? "Heyyyy friend!" Tricee answered excitedly. "Hey girl," I replied in a dry tone.

"Ewww, what's wrong with you? You just came back from the biggest conference ever as a keynote speaker, and you're sounding like you are one of the depressed audience members. What's wrong?" she asked, in a concerned tone. "My life sucks! I am so unhappy. I mean, there was news cameras there, flashing lights, and everything I have ever wanted, but I still feel unhappy," I admitted sadly. "You've got the career you've worked so hard to build, a good husband, beautiful children, and money. I mean, what more could you possibly want?" she asked me in a serious tone.

For Pastor Tucker to answer the phone when I call him, is what I thought to myself. "I know for sure that I want things with Leon to go back to how they used to be. I want him to love me like he used to. I want us to travel together and take trips with the kids. I just want everything that I don't have at this point," I admitted sadly. "I just want everything you do have at this point. Girl, you need to shut up and count ya blessings," Tricee snapped at me.

"I mean, your life could be way worse. You could be me. No man, no kids, no house, no big money," Tricee reminded me. "Girl my life is boring. I'm the one that should be complaining, but I'm not. Even though it's not what I want it to be, I count it all joy, and I thank God for it. Things can always be worse in both of our lives, ya know bestie?" Tricee said. "Yeah, I guess you're right. Thank you for reminding me of how blessed I am, as I often forget," I admitted. "Stay from round me wit ya 'woe is me attitude,' it doesn't look good on you," Tricee said playfully.

"Yes, you're right. Thanks for the pep talk bestie," I said. "Let's get back to this little boring life that you got though. I got somebody in mind for you," I told Tricee. "Chile boo, it can't be no one that we both know, cuz I have no interest in any man that I already know," Tricee said. "That's ya problem, you don't know how to think outside of the box. And for your information, it is somebody you already know, and he fineeee," I said excitedly. "Now I know you lying, cuz none of the men I know will make it to the fineeee category," Tricee snapped back.

"Well, this one is guaranteed to make the cut," I said. "Who?" Tricee asked curiously. "Johnny," I blurted out. "Johnny who?" Tricee asked, sounding confused. "Pastor Johnny, preacher Johnny, PBJ, you know, ya other Pastor," I replied sarcastically. "Oh, you tried it," Tricee said to me, as we both laughed. "What's wrong with Johnny?" I asked. "First of all, he's a preacher. You told me that Leon was boring. What makes you think I want to be with his boring best friend?" Tricee asked me.

"Oohhh no you didn't! And you wonder why I kept my marital issues a secret for so long, cuz I knew it was only gonna be a matter of time before you started throwing shade," I replied. "Shut up, you know I'm just playing," Tricee said to me. "Why him out of all people?" Tricee asked. You look good, he's handsome, and y'all can put all y'all fineness together and give me some beautiful God babies," I said excitedly.

"Interesting," Tricee said. "I don't even know if he'd be interested in a sinner like me. I'm a freak, I cuss, and I like to have a good time. I refuse to get with a man that won't let me be me. Hell, that's part of the reason I've been single for so long, because every man I get tries to change me," Tricee said. "Johnny likes to have fun too, but he's just a preacher. I think y'all would work out well together," I said confidently.

"Plus, Leon told me that you're all he's been talking about," I told Tricee. "Oh yeah? What exactly is he saying?" Tricee asked me. "He's been telling Leon how fine you are, and how he likes your smile. He said he was going to ask you out on a date, but he needs to build up his nerves to ask you," I told Tricee.

"He has to build up his nerves to ask me? He sounds like a punk to me," Tricee said as she was laughing. "He ain't a punk chile, he's just intimidated to approach a beautiful woman. I mean, can you blame him?" I asked. "Yea, I guess you're right. I am kinda like a big deal," Tricee said, as we both burst into laughter.

"So what's his story? He's a good-looking man. Why he don't have no girl?" Tricee asked. "The last girl that he had broke his heart. She did him really bad. He told me that he really loved her, but she just dumped him after they had spent years together. They were planning to get married and everything. Apparently, the girl left him, got married, and had kids with somebody else. He's been scarred ever since," I told her.

"Dang, that's messed up," Tricee said. "He needs a woman like you to make him smile and laugh again, and to show him a good time. He needs someone like you to soften his heart and cause him to love again. Plus, he'd be an excellent father. He's our kids Godfather, and he's so good with them. If you didn't know us, you'd think that Johnny is my kids' father, and Leon is the Godfather," I told Tricee.

"Well that's good to know, cuz I'm jive ready for some kids. And I'm definitely ready to have fun doing what's required to make them," Tricee said jokingly. "That's cuz you a hoe," I replied jokingly.

"Anywho, back to you and Pretty Boy Johnny," I said, changing the subject. "Is it ok if I let him know you'd be willing to go out with him?" I asked Tricee. "Yeah, why not. It's not like I have a line of qualified suitors kicking my door down," she replied. "You're crazy chick," I said, as we both laughed hysterically. "I love you too, and I'll talk to you later," Tricee told me just before she hung up.

Chapter 19

"I'M SO GLAD that we are finally getting together," Johnny told Tricee. "When Yoshi told me that you were interested in me, I was actually flattered," he said. "Well that's funny, because Yoshi told me that you were interested in me. Wait until I see her. I'm going to cuss her out something good," Tricee said laughing.

"Oh, so what you're saying is that I don't need to be flattered after all?" he asked jokingly. "Oh no, please be flattered. I think that you're a handsome man, and regardless of the lie that was told to both of us to get here, we're here. And I don't think that's a bad thing," Tricee said, as she was smiling at Johnny.

"So, I see you every Sunday at church, and I must admit that you're beautiful. To cut to the chase, what is a woman as beautiful as you still doing single?" he asked, with a confused look on his face. "To be honest, I just haven't found anybody. I love myself too much to just settle for anything and anybody, so until I can get who and what I want, I choose to remain single," Tricee answered.

"Well that's a wonderful answer. I love a woman who knows what she wants, and won't settle for less until she gets it. I completely under-stand what you're saying," he replied. "How about you? I mean, you are fine Pastor, and you're definitely in demand," Tricee said. "In demand? I wouldn't call it that. I mean, I don't just have women that are knocking my door down to get to me," he said, while laughing.

"Well I'm a woman, and women talk, and believe you me, you have been the subject of many conversations over time. Can I let you in on a little secret?" Tricee asked him. "Your secret is safe with me," he replied.

"It's not your door that they want to knock down," she whispered to him, if you know what I mean. They both busted out in laughter, as he was blushing and turning red due to being embarrassed. You're blushing," she said seductively. "Yeah, I guess I am," he replied jokingly.

"My bad Pastor, I'm a hot mess, and I don't have no filter. I apologize for even saying that to you. It was wrong and inappropriate. I didn't mean to say that to your holy ears," she said. "Girl, please stop with that craziness. Just because I'm a Pastor, doesn't mean that I don't like to have fun. At the end of the day when I take off my robe, I'm still a man in the flesh. So please don't ever try to tone down who you are just to please me and my 'holy' ears. I'm here for the Holy Spirit, but I'm also here for the foolishness," he said, while laughing.

"Wow, it's refreshing to hear you say that," Tricee said. "What's that?" he asked. "Don't tone down who I am to mesh with others. I find that to be one of the major reasons as to why me and relationships don't work, because men want me to be someone who I'm not," Tricee admitted. "I find that because I'm a Pastor, women don't show me their true selves. They try to be who they think I want them to be. That's so fake to me, and I can't stand it. Just be who you are," he said.

"I love the fact that you just stated the real, how you truly felt. I don't get that when dealing with women nowadays, because they're trying to uphold me to an image that I don't even hold myself to outside of the pulpit," he said, as if he was frustrated. "Not saying that I'm out here living recklessly or anything like that, but there's a time to be holy, and then there's a time for me to get loose and have fun," Tricee said, in a flirty manner.

"You have no idea as to how much I'm enjoying this conversation with you. Just your conversation alone has me open like a book, and

I'm digging the hell out of you," he admitted to her. "So, what's your story? Why is a handsome man that appears to be a good prospect still single? Have you had any long-term relationships or anything like that?" Tricee asked Johnny. She already knew because Yoshi told her, but she wanted to see how he was going to respond.

"Well I did back some years ago. I guess at the end of the day, the person that I loved didn't love me. My significant other left me to go be with the person that they loved," he said sadly. "Wow, I'm so sorry to hear that. It looks like to me she lost out on a good thing, and I'm bout to come scoop you right on up," Tricee said confidently. "It's life. Things happen. You live, you learn, and you move on," he said.

"Do you think that's stopped you from moving forward?" she asked. "No, not at all. I just haven't found anyone who is worthy to move forward with, and that was the last relationship that had any meaning or any substance to me," he answered. "So, if you did find a woman that you like or that you feel is worthy, would you be willing to move forward, get married and have a family?" Tricee asked hesitantly.

"Oh absolutely! Ultimately, that's what I want. But again, I'm not going to just go for anybody just to say that I have someone," he said boldly. "Wow! It seems like we have a lot in common. I'm just going to be honest with you and tell you that I like what I'm seeing and hearing, and I love what I'm smelling. My panties are soaking wet," she said excitedly.

"Wait, did you say your panties are wet?" he asked, as if he was disgusted. "I'm so sorry Pastor, did I say the wrong thing?" she asked, in a concerned tone. "Hell naw, you ain't say nothing wrong. I was just hoping that you didn't have any panties on at all. I don't like having anything in the way when it's time to drink 'water from the well,' if you know what I mean," he said. "Well, let me tell you that the fountain is ready to be drunk from, and it's free flowing," she replied.

He moved over next to her, grabbed her face, and started kissing her passionately right in the middle of the restaurant. "Excuse me, would you all like to place your order?" the waiter asked, interrupting the passionate moment. "No, we've actually changed our mind. We'll just come back later," he said, as he took her hand and led her out of the restaurant. On the way out of the restaurant, they hugged and kissed as if they were teenagers in love.

"Come over to my truck," he said. She followed behind him as he guided her to the truck. They both got in, and he drove to a dark parking lot where they begin kissing again. He stuck his hand up under her dress, and felt her bare butt and pussy. "You don't got no panties on," he said, as he stopped kissing her. "Fooled you," she said, while laughing.

He took his fingers and slid them in and out of her a few times. He then put his fingers in his mouth and said, "You taste better than I ever imagined you would. I mean, I knew you would taste good, but you taste 'good good.' Lay down on the back seat," he commanded. She was hot, horny, and liked the direction she was being led to, so she complied. He pulled her body down towards the edge of the seat, opened her legs, and satisfied her with his mouth.

He wasn't down there for a good 6 minutes, before she screamed and moaned his name before releasing herself on his beard. "Yeass!" she screamed, as she sat up feeling wet and sticky. "So did you enjoy it?" he asked her, as she was trying to wipe and fix herself up. "To say I enjoyed myself would be an understatement. I feel like I have Heaven right here on Earth with you," she replied. "I just feel so bad for nutting so quick. I'm so embarrassed," she said, placing her hands over her face.

"Don't be. Don't forget, I got this 'holy mouth,' and I'm good at what I do. Plus, I know that you're backed up, it's been a while for both of us honestly, so I forgive you, 5-minute lady," he joked with her. "Can I return the favor?" Tricee asked Johnny. "Geez, I thought you'd never ask," he said, while laughing and unbuckling his pants.

She pulled out his meat, and was in awe at how big and beautiful it was. "I don't know how I'm going to take on this challenge. You have the biggest dick I've ever seen or sucked," she admitted. "Baby girl, you can do all things through Christ that strengthens you. Go ahead and handle yours," he reminded her.

She started by licking it slowly up and down. She went to the head and licked around it. She then opened her mouth as wide as she could, and went for what she knew. She literally felt that thing down her throat, and started choking on it. That must have really been a turn on to him because as she was choking, he was moaning even harder.

All of a sudden, she felt a hot thick liquid hit the back of her throat, and he started having convulsions. *I'm going to die sucking some dick,* she thought, as she literally felt like she couldn't breathe anymore. She came off the dick, and made a big gulping noise. "Ahhhhhh," she said, as if she had just got finished drinking a cold drink on a hot summer day. "Oh my God!" he yelled. "What's wrong?" she asked. "And you swallow? Tricee, will you marry me?" he asked her in a serious tone.

"What?" she replied. "I'm for real, will you marry me? Truth be told, I've been in love with you from the first moment I laid eyes on you. And then after this conversation and what we just did, I know that you're my soulmate, and I don't want to do another day on this Earth without you," he said convincingly. "Wow, I'm speechless. I don't know what to say," she said.

"Say yes, please say yes," he said. "I can hear the conversation now when I'm sitting around with my girls telling them I'm getting married, and they ask how you proposed. I in turn tell them how I sucked your dick so good that you wanted this mouth for the rest of your life. What a romantic proposal story," she said sarcastically.

"We'll make up another story if we have to. Only me and you will know the real. Hell, I'll go buy you a ring tomorrow, please just say yes," he begged. "Yes! I'll be more than happy to be Mrs. Johnny Reals. Oh my God, I'm so excited! I've never been proposed to. I've never thought I was worthy to be married, and I'm getting married," she cried.

"You are getting married baby girl. You are going to be Mrs. Johnny Reals," he said. "What do we do from this point on?" she asked Johnny nervously. "We plan a wedding. It can be as big or as small as you want it to be. You're a special woman, and I want this day to be the most special day of your life. I want it to be the day that you've always dreamed of," he told Tricee.

They put their clothes back on, and he drove her back to her car.

You have officially made me the happiest man in the world tonight," he said, as he got out and opened her car door. "Come on and follow me. It's time for us to go home," she said seductively. "As tempting as that sounds, I don't want to get into the habit of sinning. We're going to do things the right way. You're going to your house, and I'm going to my house, but we can talk until the sun comes up," he said.

"I respect you for that, and I love that idea. God will bless our union if we do things the right way, so I'm all for it," she said, agreeing with him. "Goodnight my soon-to-be wife, he said, while smiling. "Goodnight my soon-to-be husband," she replied, as they both drove off.

Chapter 20

I LOOKED AT THE caller id on my phone as it was ringing. It read, "Best Friend" across the top of the screen. "Hey girl," I said, as I answered the phone. "Girl, guess what? Tricee excitedly said to me. "Hey girl! What's up?" I replied. "I got some good news for you!" she said excitedly. "Well I'm glad, cuz I can definitely use some good news in my life," I replied.

"Well, I took your advice, and I went out on a date with Johnny," Tricee said happily. "What? You know I need all the juicy details," I said. "Nope, I'm not giving them to you. On my date, I found out that you lied to me," Tricee said to me. "I lied to you?" I asked confusingly. "Yup. You told me that Johnny wants to get with me. Well he told me that you said I was asking about him, and wanted to get with him," Tricee said, in an irritated manner. "Yeah, and your point?" I replied sarcastically.

"You had me looking mad stupid Yosh," Tricee said. "How did I have you looking stupid?" I asked, in a confused tone. "You had me thinking I was wanted, and you had him thinking I wanted him, and neither of those were the case," she replied, in a frustrated tone. "Right, and so ya bestie did what she had to do to make it all work out, right?" I asked sarcastically. "Yea, I guess," Tricee said with an attitude.

"You have to remember, I know both of y'all really well. Had I not done what I did, you would not have this happiness in your voice that I'm hearing across my phone line now, would you?" I asked. "No, I wouldn't," Tricee admitted. "So, where's my thank you then?" I asked Tricee. "Thank you, Chick. I love you girl, and I'm sorry that I tried to get you together, only for you to get me together," Tricee said, in a guilty manner. "It's OK, just don't let it happen again," I said jokingly.

"Soooo, me and Johnny decided that we are going to get married," Tricee said happily. "I hate to sound like a Debbie Downer, but married?" I asked her. "Yes married!" Tricee said excitedly. "Ok, first of all, who thought of this, and second of all, why did y'all think this would be a good idea?" I asked. "Why do you think that it's not a good idea?" Tricee asked me, in an agitated manner.

"Ok, let's think this through. You've been knowing him on a hi/ bye basis for a little over a year now. Y'all go on a date, and in 2.2 seconds, you think you know him? Ummm yea okay," I said sarcastically. "Wowwww, I thought that out of all people, you'd be happy for me. You sounding real haterish right now Yosh," Tricee said, in a sad tone. "I guess you feel as if you're the only person that deserves happiness in the world huh?" Tricee asked sarcastically.

"No girl, it's not like that at all. You know I want you to be happy, because if I didn't, I would've stayed quiet about the hook up, and left you in ya little miserable world," I said, while laughing. "From what you've told me, I'm not the only one that's miserable," Tricee snapped back. "Ya husband don't want you, and for all you know, he can be screwing somebody else! So please don't come for me like every-thing's all good in ya life, because we both know it ain't. You told me, remember?" Tricee yelled into the phone.

"I should've trusted my first mind and never said anything to you about my marital problems," I told Tricee. "I mean, you always throwing low key shade like you ain't living in a glass house, and to be honest with you, I'm sick of it," Tricee yelled, in a frustrated tone. "I was wrong about calling your life miserable, and I'm sorry if I hurt your feelings Tricee. It's just that I think that y'all are moving too fast," I admitted.

"Like, what's his favorite color? What's his phone number? What do you really know about him?" is all I'm asking Tricee. "I know that he's fine, and I know that his mouth gave me the best orgasm that I've ever had in my life," Tricee replied. "Awww that's it, he got you open from his 'head skills,' huh?" I asked sarcastically. "I mean, I just really like him. And for your information, I don't have his phone number," Tricee admitted.

"You mean to tell me that you're about to marry a man whose phone number you gotta look up in the church directory?" I asked. "Don't do me please," she responded, as we both laughed. "So, what's the rush to the altar about?" I asked. "We want to make sure we are doing things the right way. We don't want to be out here sinning, so why not make it official, 1st lady?" Tricee asked me. "Oh, so now you got a conscious now after he gave you some good head huh? Was that not a sin? Girl bye," I said jokingly.

"Yo, what is up with you? I would think you, the '1st Lady' would understand wanting to live right, and doing things right in the sight of God. I'm mad confused right now," Tricee said. "I just don't want y'all to make a mistake that y'all are going to regret. I love both of you, and if y'all don't work out, I will lose my brother and my sister. In all honesty, I just feel like y'all should know each other better before making such a life changing decision like getting married," I admitted.

"Is there something that I don't know about him that I should know, Yoshi?" Tricee asked me. "Not that I know of. I know he's a good solid dude. That's all I can honestly say about him," I responded. "I know what I'm doing friend. It's time to do the things in my life that make me happy, and I feel like this will make me happy," Tricee reassured me.

"What was it that you needed to talk to me about?" Tricee asked, trying to change the subject. "Oh nothing major. I don't want to take away from your moment Tricee. Congratulations, and just know that I'm here for you both," I said, half-heartedly. "That's more like it, be happy for me," Tricee said.

"Hell, we got a wedding to plan, and I'll be sure to invite some well-endowed strippers to your bachelorette party. It's always nice to see, 'the Lord's creations,' yes lawwdd," I said jokingly. "You so nasty," Tricee said, while laughing. "Well get to planning, cuz I'm ready to see those 'mighty wonders,' as well," Tricee teased back, while hanging up the phone.

Chapter 21

"**B**RUH BRUH," JOHNNY said excitedly to Leon. "What's up man?" he answered, as he walked into the church office for Wednesday night Bible study. "Why do you sound so excited?" Leon asked Johnny. "Man, you're not gonna believe what happened," Johnny said. "What? You got some of that sweet pussy meat from one of them sisters from the church?" he asked inquisitively.

"Nope, it's even better than that," Johnny replied. "What can possibly be better than sweet pussy?" he asked Johnny, looking confused. "I've met the woman for me. I'm in love!" Johnny said excitedly. "Oh yeah? I just saw you earlier this week, and you were looking down in the dumps. Now you're in love?" he asked Johnny. "Yep, and it gets even better. We're getting married!" Johnny said joyfully.

"Married? You don't think you're moving a little bit too fast bro?" Leon asked Johnny. "Nope, I sure don't," Johnny replied. "Well who is the lucky lady? Anybody I know?" Leon asked. "Yes, you know her," Johnny said. "Who is she? What does she look like?" Leon asked Johnny. "Tricee from church," Johnny admitted. "My Tricee, Yoshi's best friend Tricee?" Leon asked Johnny. "Yep, that's my lady," Johnny said proudly. "Wow, I can't believe this," Leon said while laughing.

"Can't believe what? From the look on your face, you're not happy about this," Johnny told Leon.

"You damn right I'm not happy about it," Leon yelled. "I'm confused. I just knew that you'd be happy for me. You're always telling me to get some pussy and to find a wife. I finally get someone who I love and who loves me, and you call yourself being mad," Johnny said to Leon, with a look of confusion on his face.

"I can't believe you man," Leon said, cracking his knuckles. "Damn man, I don't understand what the problem is," he said to Leon. "You betrayed me man," Leon said angrily to Johnny. "Betrayed?" Johnny asked, looking for clarification. "Yes, I said what I meant. We had a conversation about the ladies in the church, and I specifically told you not to bother her, because I wanted her for myself. I told you that she was the forbidden fruit, and that you were free to have anybody else other than her," Leon reminded Johnny.

"Aww man you trippin! I'm supposed to pass up on marrying a beautiful woman because of your wack ass fantasy? Man fuck you and your fantasy," Johnny said, laughing at Leon. "Man, you're married to Yoshi," Johnny reminded Leon. "How are you going to get mad at me, a single man for getting with a single woman, and you're married?

Not only are you married, but you're a married Pastor. Not only are you a married Pastor, your wife is the best friend of the woman that we are speaking of. Am I missing something here? Are you fucking her or something, because if not, you should definitely have no issues with me marrying her. So please tell me what's really going on?" Johnny asked Leon.

"In real life, we've never messed around, but in my head, hell yeah we've messed around. In my dreams, I've had sex with her so many times. I mean, I've been feenin for that woman. I was planning on making my move on her any day now. It wouldn't be right for you to marry her bro. Why would you want to marry someone that your best friend fantasizes and lusts about all day and night?" Leon asked Johnny. "I just can't turn my feelings for her off like that, and to be honest, I don't want to," Leon admitted.

"Well bro, I'm sorry. This is a battle that you will not win. I'd suggest you pray about the situation. Pray those lustful, sinful feelings up off of you, because you or nobody else is going to stop me from marrying that woman," Johnny said, as he stormed out of the office.

Chapter 22

"BROTHERS AND SISTERS, I'm here to remind you today that you need to be blameless," Pastor Leon yelled from the pulpit during Wednesday night Bible study. If you open your Bibles to the book of Philippians, Chapter 2 Verse 15, it reads, "That ye may be blameless and harmless, the sons of God, without rebuke, in the midst of a crooked and perverse nation, among whom ye shine as lights in the world," Pastor Leon read.

"We can't walk around here doing any and everything with any and everybody. How can we be considered blameless if we're around here dibbling and dabbling in mess that we shouldn't be involved in?" he asked convincingly. "Me personally, you're not gonna catch me out here slipping and sliding, because I know all about that 'All Seeing Eye.' We just can't get away from it, and being that I know it's watching me, it will watch me doing the right thing at all times." he said. "I hope y'all feel the same way," Pastor Leon shouted, as the members clapped and said Amen!

"I am the leader of this flock. I am held accountable for your souls, and I will not lead you all to hell. If you're going to follow me, you're going to follow me up the Stairway of Heaven. Every once in a while, as your Pastor, I have to have difficult conversations with you all. I'm bringing this to your attention because I'm hearing and seeing a lot of things. A lot of people are creeping and sneaking, and simply put, a lot of people aren't living Christ like lives," Pastor Leon said.

"Amennnn," a brother yelled from the audience. "I see Deacon Johnson agrees with me. "Thank you, brother," Pastor Leon said. "Y'all know I don't like having these conversations, but your blood is on my hands. And if I'm living right and I'm accountable for y'all soul's, y'all are going to be living right too," he said.

"We have got to stop this foolishness," he said, looking at Pastor Johnny with evil eyes. "Amen walls, cuz y'all have gotten quiet on me," he shouted. "I will not continue to let brothers work in the Lord's church if you all are not doing right by your wives and your children. Some of you sit around, watch TV, and play video games all day, while your wives go to work, and then have to come home and take care of you.

The house is dirty, the clothes need to be folded, no food has been cooked, but yet, you want to be called a man. Then you want to come complain to me because she's not letting you be the head of the house. Some of y'all ain't nothing but a joke," he admitted. "To be honest with you, if I was a woman, you wouldn't be able to lead me either. A lot of you are nothing but breath in britches," he said, as he busted out in laughter.

Y'all spending your wife's hard-earned money down there at the casino's. Your wives are having to come to the church so we can pay the light bill because you're out here giving her hard-earned money to these 'Jezebel' women of the world. Y'all ought to be ashamed of yourselves," Pastor Leon yelled to the audience.

"And I know y'all don't think that Pastor knows, but a lot of you have stepped out on your wives," he stated. "Preach it preacha!" Brother Johnson yelled from the audience again. "Do you not realize that your wives are a gift from God? I wouldn't dare think about stepping out on my wife. If I step out on my beloved, who is God's child, I know I'll have to deal with her Daddy, and I'm not ready for that heat," Pastor Leon admitted.

"I love my wife. She has given me a beautiful home, and beautiful children. I mean honestly, what more can a man ask for? I'd be a fool to do anything that would dishonor, disrespect, and embarrass her, because she is me. And we all know I love myself, and I will never do anything to hurt myself, and I won't do anything to hurt her," Pastor said, as he was wrapping up his message.

"Simply put Saints, we have got to get it together. God is not pleased with the things that are going on, and quite honestly, I'm not either. I'm holding you accountable for the things that are being done, because I love you, and I refuse to let you send me to hell, especially when I'm living right in the eyes of the Lord," he reminded the Saints.

"At this time, I want to let you know that the doors of the church are open. If you need to repent and get your life right with God, please do so now," Pastor Leon said, as he was walking out of the pulpit. "Good job bro," Johnny said to Leon. Leon rolled his eyes at Johnny as he walked back to his office.

Chapter 23

PASTOR LEON WALKED into his office and closed the door. He noticed the shadow of someone strikingly beautiful sitting down in his counseling chair. "Kat, what are you doing here?" he asked angrily. "You know what I'm doing here Pastor," she replied seductively. "I loved your message this evening sir, she told Pastor Leon. "Well thank you Kat," he replied. "What's wrong with you?" she asked him. "I got some news earlier that really made me upset, and the fact that you're here after I told you I don't want to deal with you or your foolishness any longer, is making me even more angry!" he yelled.

She stood up, opened up her long pea coat which bore her naked body, and watched him as he marveled upon her with lust in his eyes. She went up and whispered in his ear while grabbing his manhood, and said, "You're right, we do have to stop this foolishness," as she guided his hands all over her voluptuous body. She got down on her knees and started unbuckling his belt. "Can I do what I love to do to you?" she asked, while pulling his pants down.

"You have crossed the line," he said angrily. "My wife is out there, my kids are out there, and the people who follow me as their leader are out there as well," he reminded her. "And I'm here," she said, in a sexy voice. "Tell me you don't want me here, and I'll willfully leave," she said. "I don't, I mean, I do want you here. We're taking a big chance by being here," he reminded her.

"If you'd just shut up and give me 2 minutes to do what I want to do, you can leave and go greet your flock," Kat said seductively. Pastor put his face in his hands, and after a few sucks from Kat, he gave Kat what she wanted.

"Oh my God, I can't believe that this just happened, and it just happened here. You have to promise me that this will never ever happen again," he said to her. "Oh, it'll happen again, just not here, if it was really that bad," she said sadly. "I mean, it wasn't bad at all," he admitted. "It was real good, just kind of scary. My heart was pounding the whole time," he admitted. "That's what makes it so fun," she said, as they both laughed.

"Walk out of my office. If anyone sees and questions you, especially Yoshi, just let her know that you needed to speak to me about an important decision," he told Kat. "Close the door," Pastor yelled, as she tried to discreetly leave his office. As she was walking out, the first face she saw was Deacon Johnson's. "I want next, and by the way, don't forget to wipe the nut off your mouth before Yoshi sees it," he said while laughing. She hung her head down, and ran to the bathroom in embarrassment.

While in the bathroom, she put her head down to gather herself, as she felt tears forming in the back of her eyes. She looked up at the reflection of herself in the mirror in shame, and she did have semen around her mouth, and just as Brother Johnson suggested, she wiped it off her mouth before Yoshi could see it.

Chapter 24

"WELL HELLO," DEACON Johnson said to Pastor, as he opened the office door without knocking. Pastor looked quite embarrassed, as Brother Johnson sat there and watched him fix his belt. "Good afternoon Sir. I'm sorry, I didn't hear you knock on the door," Pastor said sarcastically. "Yep, that's because I didn't," Deacon Johnson replied, with equally as much sarcasm.

"Do I feel some tension in the air?" Pastor Leon asked Deacon Johnson. "No, no tension at all, but there is something that's been bothering me though, in all honesty Pastor," he replied. "What's going on my brother?" Pastor asked in a concerned tone.

"I've admired and looked up to you as my spiritual Father for years now. The last time that I saw you, you were in a compromising position. I tried to overlook it, and give you the benefit of the doubt, but now I know that what I was speculating is true," Deacon Johnson told Pastor. "And what exactly would the truth be?" Pastor Leon asked curiously.

"That you are a wolf in sheep's clothing, and a hypocrite," Deacon Johnson stated boldly. "You just sat up and preached to your flock about being 'blameless,' yet you are guilty of doing the same things that you were calling us out on doing. Were you speaking from a guilty conscious Pastor?" Brother Johnson asked him. "Excuse me?" Pastor Leon shouted at him. "I said what I said, I didn't stutter. I know that you are sleeping with that woman. The question is, does your wife know?" Deacon Johnson asked Pastor.

"Know what? That I'm an innocent man? That I do things in accordance with God's will? That I value my family and this church family, and that I won't do anything to lose the good things that I have in my life?" Pastor Leon asked. "Right, all of that," Deacon Johnson said, while laughing. "What's so funny?" Pastor Leon asked in an agitated manner.

"You know, the day I caught you with your hand in the cookie jar, you were fumbling out of that woman's house all confused and scared looking, kind of like the same way you're looking now. I mean, you were looking like you saw a ghost the moment you saw me, and once again, I gave you the benefit of the doubt like an idiot. Everything still didn't look right to me though, so I went to her house after you pulled off," Brother Johnson admitted.

"I asked her what you were doing there. She told me you all were having a Bible study. When I asked you what you were doing there, you said that you were planning a surprise birthday party for your wife, not remembering that your wife's birthday was on a Sunday a few months ago, and you had me deliver flowers to her. So, one of y'all is lying, and my good sense is telling me that it's both of y'all," Deacon Johnson boldly proclaimed.

"Don't come in here with this foolishness," Pastor yelled. "You have no proof that this has occurred, and I will sue you for slander, if I have to. I will NOT have my family, my reputation, and most importantly my church, be put under scrutiny due to these false accusations," Pastor Leon yelled, while pointing his finger in Deacon Johnson's face. "Oh, actually I do. Look at this," he said confidently. He handed Pastor Leon his phone, which he looked at in shock.

Play by play, moment by moment, he saw himself leaving out of Kat's house with his clothes in disarray. "Does this look familiar?" Deacon Johnson asked Pastor Leon. "No it doesn't, I have no idea who this is, but I do know that it's not me," Pastor Leon said confidently.

"And even if it was me, that's not me," he said arrogantly, while deleting the video from Deacon Johnson's phone, and handing it back to him.

"How dare you delete something that rightfully belongs to me?" Brother Johnson asked. "You may have deleted this video here, but you definitely can't delete this video here," he told Pastor Leon. "What video are you talking about now, Pastor Leon asked curiously, as Deacon Johnson handed him his phone again. He saw a replay of the events that occurred not even 30 minutes prior. A beautiful woman who was not Pastor's wife, slobbin his knob. Pastor deleted that video as well, and gave Brother Johnson his phone back.

"It's a good thing I have a backup of these videos, or I wouldn't have a leg to stand on to prove my case, now would I Pastor?" he asked Leon. "The good thing about this video here is it's on file with the alarm company," Deacon Johnson reminded Pastor. "Everybody from the alarm company is probably watching you in that sexual act, so this is bigger than me and you. When one of the underpaid employees realize that this was done in a church, they'll leak it to one of the major news/social media outlets anyway, so you actually need me if you want this to go away," he said.

"I manage the alarm account, as it's paid with my personal funds. The username and password were created by me, so you'll never be able to guess it," Deacon Johnson advised Pastor in a serious tone. "Please see yourself out," Pastor Leon said, dismissing Deacon. "Oh you finished, because I'm not?" Deacon Johnson asked Pastor. "Yes, you are finished," Pastor told him, as he went and opened the door for Deacon Johnson to leave.

"I'm gonna leave, but I want you to know that your sins have found you out, and this isn't the last that you're going to hear about this," he shouted at Pastor, as he stormed out. "You threatening me?" Pastor asked angrily, while following Brother Johnson. "No, it's not a threat, it's a promise. But, I'm a fair man. I'm willing to let all of this go, but it's going to come with a price," he said connivingly.

"A price?" Pastor Leon asked confusingly. "Yes, a price," Deacon Johnson replied. "How much are you talking?" Pastor Bowens asked inquisitively. "$500,000, and you'll never hear from me again, Deacon

Johnson said, as he walked back into Pastor's office. "What the fuck!" Pastor yelled, while closing the door. You know in the hell well that I don't have that type of money," he said.

"Pastor, have you forgotten that I'm on the board of treasury, and I know how much money this church brings in every single Sunday? Last week the church bought in over $28,000. Easter Sunday, we bought in $72,000, that's $100,000 of my $500,000 right there. As you've told me before, you're a very smart man, so therefore, you can figure out how to get me the rest of my money," he said sarcastically.

"Not this church here," Pastor replied confidently, as he logged on to the computer to pull up the offering logs. Pastor Johnny has it reported here that last week we collected a little less than $2,500.00," Pastor Leon said. "Both Pastor Johnny and I were here counting the offering, and it was over $28,000 there," Deacon Johnson said confidently.

"There must be some type of mistake," Pastor Leon said. "I don't think that there was a mistake that was made. But it does sound like you aren't the only person who has some secrets in the fold. Wow, what do you think the Saints would say about all of these findings?" Deacon Johnson asked sarcastically.

"There must be a mistake," Pastor Leon said to Deacon Johnson. "Yep, probably like the mistaken identity and the person who isn't you in the videos, but some burdens aren't my burdens to bear. As a matter of fact, I want $10,000.00 of it within the next hour," Brother Johnson demanded. "Where do you expect me to get that type of money from in the next hour?" Pastor asked Deacon.

"Hell if I know. Go in your savings account. Hell, go back in the collection plate. I don't care where you get it from, I just know I want my money. The clock is ticking, starting now!" Deacon Johnson said sarcastically, as he walked out of Pastor's office. Pastor then went and closed the door behind him. He dropped his head into his hands. "*Satan, where did you come from?*" he thought to himself, as if he weren't Satan in the flesh.

Chapter 25

AFTER EVERYONE LEFT, Johnny came back in the office where Leon had been sitting in his pity, feeling heavy hearted. "Hey man, let me holla at you," Pastor Leon said to Johnny, before he could sit down. "I don't even like ya tone, so I hope this ain't got nothing to do with me and Tricee getting married," Johnny replied defensively.

"Nah, this is bigger than a bitch," Leon replied sarcastically. "First of all, I'm not going to let you disrespect my fiancé bro. You're dead wrong for that. Never once have I disrespected Yosh, even when she was acting like a bitch. I would hate to have to fall out with you over this, but please believe, I will," Johnny said in a serious tone.

"Let's cut to the chase. Have you been stealing money from the church?" Leon asked Johnny. "What? How dare you accuse me of this?" Johnny yelled. "I didn't accuse you of anything, but you do start sounding like you're guilty when you start mistaking a question for an accusation," Leon said sternly. "I don't even understand why you would come at me like this.

I've known you for years, and you've never known me to be a thief. You can say a lot of things about me, but thief is not one of them.

Where's all this coming from?" Johnny asked Leon. "It's been brought to my attention that thousands of dollars are being stolen from the church every Sunday, and it's only four of us that have access to the money. Me, you, Yoshi, and Deacon Johnson," Leon said.

"Well hell, did you ask them? It's not like he has the best reputation around here," Johnny reminded Leon. "He's the one who alerted me to the situation, so I know it's not him," Leon said confidently. "I hate to say it, but did you ask Yoshi?" Johnny asked Leon. "Yoshi wouldn't dare do this. There are some things that I won't even bring to her attention, and this is one of them," Leon said defensively.

"So, you just gon automatically blame me huh? I can't believe this man! I think that you're trying to throw dirt against my 'blameless name,' being that I'm marrying the woman of your dreams. If that's what you're trying to do, believe me, it's not going to work," Johnny said sarcastically.

"I'm going to get to the bottom of this, and when I do, there's going to be hell to pay," Leon threatened. "Speak now, so that we can resolve this issue quietly amongst us," Leon told Johnny. "The truth always prevails," Johnny said, as he logged into the church's bank account.

"I see that there was a cash app transaction recently to somebody by the name of 'Mzwetpussy?' Would you happen to know anything about that?" Johnny asked Leon. "I don't know what you're talking about. I don't even have cash app, nor do I use it," Leon replied confidently.

"Thank you for bringing this to my attention, as I'll now be going over the church's treasury records with a fine-tooth comb as well. As I'm doing some further researching here, it was your user ID and password that was used to make the transaction on that day," Johnny said confidently.

"You got some damn nerve accusing me of stealing, and you out here paying for pussy with the church's money. Or did you forget about that before you started throwing stones?" Johnny asked Leon sarcastically. "That's impossible, someone must have compromised my username and password. I don't pay for pussy, and if I would be so foolish to do so, I wouldn't use the church's money to do it with," Leon yelled defensively. "You know, they say the same hole that you try to dig for others is the same hole that you'll find your feet sticking up out of. This is a dirty game that you're playing, and I just hope that you're ready to lose," Pastor Johnny said seriously, as he walked out of the office to leave the building for the night.

"Dang, what's wrong with you?" I asked Johnny, as he stormed pass me and the kids as Kylie reached out to hug him. "Your husband has lost his damn mind. You need to talk some sense into him, cuz he's tripping for real," he replied angrily. "Okay, I will," I said, as the kids and I walked back into the office. "Bae, what's going on with you and Johnny? I just saw him, and he's super upset. What's up with y'all?" I asked curiously.

"I had to call him out on a few things, and you know people don't like being called out. I guess he's in his feelings. Prayerfully, he'll get over it sooner than later, and repent," Leon told me. "You're looking awfully beautiful today honey," Leon said, while changing the subject. "Well thank you baby. I try to stay looking good for you, you know. I'm just glad you noticed me again," I responded.

"Well, you're not trying, you're doing," he reminded me. "I can't wait until we get home, so I can make love to my wife," he said to me passionately. "Oh yeah, tell me more," I said. "Ewwww, y'all nasty," the kids said while laughing. Leon motioned for me and the kids, and we all shared a big family hug, before we were interrupted by Deacon Johnson.

"Hey Sister Bowens, how are you doing? Please excuse me for a minute, I need to have a minute with your husband," he said sharply, not giving me the opportunity to respond to his question. "Sure thing, but don't take too long. We have some business to handle," I said, while winking my eye. "Oh, I understand. I know that Pastor is a man that likes to handle his business," he said sarcastically.

"I promise this isn't going to take long at all," he said. "Can we ride home with you Daddy?" JJ asked Leon. "Sure, you can son, y'all just go wait in the hallway for me while I talk to Deacon Johnson," he said. I went and gave Leon a hug and kiss, and headed out. "You got my money?" Deacon Johnson asked Leon, in a serious tone.

"You said you would give me an hour, and it's only been about a half an hour," Pastor reminded Deacon, after looking at his watch. "Time is up Pastor. I want my money now!" Deacon Johnson demanded. "Simply put, I got money, but I don't got no money to give you, so handle things as you may. I refuse to bribed," Pastor Leon said to Deacon. "So be it," Deacon said angrily, as he left out of the office.

Leon and the kids straightened up the sanctuary and cleaned the church for 30 minutes before heading home. As Leon drove home, the kids fell asleep. The silence started bothering him, so he called Yoshi, and her phone went to voicemail. With what felt like the weight of the world on his shoulders, Leon started to pray.

"Dear Lord,

How did I get here? Why did I think that I was the exception to the rule? I know better than what I'm doing. I know better than what I've done. I've got myself into some mess that quite honestly, I don't know how I'm going to get out of. I wish I would have avoided the very appearance of evil, but instead, I ran to it. I have destroyed my life Lord, and I'm so sorry for my actions.

In the name of Jesus,

I pray,

Amen."

He pulled up to the house, and noticed Yoshi's car wasn't there yet. As he parked the car and started walking in the house, Yoshi sent a video message to him. *There goes my baby*, he thought to himself while opening the message.

To his surprise, he saw a blindfolded Yoshi screaming and crying. Another message followed the video message stating, "$10,000.00 BY 9AM TOMORROW MORNING, OR YOU'LL NEVER SEE YOUR WIFE AGAIN. GET THE POLICE INVOLVED, AND YOU'LL NEVER SEE YOUR WIFE AGAIN.

P.S. THIS IS NOT A GAME!!!!!

Made in the USA
Coppell, TX
19 January 2020